Sergeant's Business and Other Stories

Also from John D. Beatty

Fiction

Crop Duster: A Novel of World War II

The Liberty Bell Files: J. Edgar's Demons

The Stella's Game Trilogy
Stella's Game: A Story of Friendships
Tideline: Friendship Abides
The Safe Tree: Friendship Triumphs

Non-Fiction
The Devil's Own Day: Shiloh and the American Civil War
Why the Samurai Lost Japan: A Study in Miscalculation and Folly
(with Lee Rochwerger)

A Sun Tzu Companion

Sergeant's Business and Other Stories

John D. Beatty

•JDB•COMMUNICATIONS,•LLC•

JDB Communications, LLC

West Allis, Wisconsin

Second Paperback Edition ISBN 978-1-7347952-4-0
Second E-Book Edition ISBN 978-1-7347952-5-7

A version of *The Charge* appeared in the November 1995 issue of *Dream Forge* and the April 1996 issue of *Ebb and Flow*.

A version of *Moles* appeared in the May 1996 issue of *Nrv8*.

A version of *Marbury Rose* appeared in the January 1996 issue of *Dream Forge*.

A version of *Old Salt* appeared in the Winter 1994 issue of *The International Journal of Military Fiction*. Another version was published in the June 1996 issue of *MAKAR*.

A version of *What Happened* appeared in the Spring 1996 issue of *Ebbing Tide*.

A version of *Buddies* appeared in the April 1996 edition of *Staaxx*.

Scots Wa Hae
Lyrics by Robert Burns ca 1793

Taps
Lyrics attributed to Horace Lorenzo Trim, date unknown
Melody attributed to Dan Butterfield ca. 1862

For Frank...
*My unstoppable, unflappable, irresistible, inscrutable, and hirsute
editor, lunch companion, verbal sparring partner, fellow veteran.
and
friend for more years than either of us cares to remember...
accurately.*

And his Child-Bride Joann...
Who has put up with both of us for longer than she wants to remember.

Contents

Foreword

> ***The universe is so vast and so ageless***
> ***That the life of one man can only be justified***
> ***By the measure of his sacrifice.***

> ***-- V.A. Rosewarn, 1940***

This collection is about the unsung, the innumerable heroes who don't get into the history books. These heroes struggle on many levels and are hurt and killed by the elements, bad luck and stupidity, and sometimes by life's ultimate absurdity.

Those of you looking for hidden insights into the author's life through these stories…a writer has to be many things to do his job well, and masking himself is counterproductive. *All* stories contain little pieces of their creator. I feel compelled to share these pictures and the voices in my head for reasons I have trouble describing, so I won't trouble *you* with those thoughts.

So, enjoy...

John D. Beatty
West Allis, Wisconsin
2021

Sergeant's Business

I humbly present a primer for those of you who DON'T know what a sergeant IS or what they DO.

Billy Dent wasn't sure of the sound he heard, but something told him he should look south. He saw wisps of *something* in the soft mist over the dense trees…air currents dancing in the early morning glow. Not quite right for a Tennessee morning in April.

The battery was still waking up on that early Sunday morning. The first inspection and drill weren't supposed to be for another hour, and the men were at their breakfast. But the *sound* made Dent uneasy.

"Captain Arbor," Dent called, "Sir, if I could trouble you for a moment?" Battery Commander Richard Arbor was in his shirtsleeves, barely awake and rubbing his face. He pulled up his suspenders as he slowly walked to where Dent was in the tall meadow grass.

"Yes, what *is* it, Sergeant Dent?" Before the war, Arbor had been an attorney in Peoria. Though he respected Dent's views, they were often inconvenient and at odds with his own. Like most volunteer officers, he was uncertain just *why* the Regular NCOs like Dent were sent to the volunteer units. But Dent *had* made his battery one of the most-drilled, if not *the* best-drilled, in this army.

"With respect, sir, Do *you* hear something? Over by that treeline there?" Arbor stooped, squinting slightly. When he did that, Dent always thought the battery commander looked like an owl.

"Why, um..." Arbor squinted again, harder this time, turning his head slightly. "That...swirling in the mist over there. What *is* that?"

"I don't *know*, sir," Dent replied. "They *say* the Rebels aren't around here, so..."

"*They* can be wrong, Sergeant," Arbor said. Unlike many of his contemporaries, Arbor didn't always trust what his superiors told him. "Wasn't there a picket fight last night?" Arbor's face cleared as he adjusted his suspenders. He started glancing around the meadow, ignoring a growing number of his command who were suddenly interested in the south treeline.

Arbor knew something of his senior sergeant, though not much. He knew he'd been in uniform practically since he was born, had had frontier schooling, and an appointment to West Point, but for some reason, he'd stayed a sergeant. When Arbor had raised a company of volunteers and marched them to the camp, they just made him a captain, and it seemed natural to him. Why someone would not want to be an officer was a mystery. But Arbor knew that Dent's sole purpose in life seemed to be to get men to serve the guns, and he also knew that he did that *very* well indeed—better than any he'd ever known of or seen.

"Get the *teams* hitched up, Sergeant Dent," Arbor said finally. "Get the center section over behind that tree stand to the north. Get the trains into the woodline behind it. Set up the left and right sections on either side once they're in place."

"Yessir," Dent replied, turning to the encampment behind him. "Awright, you hooligans, you *heard* the captain; *get* it up, *pack* it up. Suddenly the men were dousing fires, rolling up bedrolls, shaking out tack, and otherwise moving in the barely organized confusion of a six-gun battery preparing to move. Arbor started shouting orders to his officers, and one young lieutenant cantered off in the direction of the Indiana infantry regiment on the right, and another to the Illinois regiment to the left. "*Guns* and *caissons*. Hitch up those *teams* there. *Move* it, boys, *come* on…"

Half the battery's two hundred horses were hitched in just a few moments when someone shouted. "Are those *Rebs*?" Dent swirled about to the south and beheld, not five hundred yards away, a long, sinuous line of brown and gray men emerging from the trees and moving steadily across the field. They seemed like a tide marching across the wet grass, muskets gleaming on their shoulders, flags rolling in the dead air as the bearers waved them back and forth. On both flanks, the infantry drums started the long roll, and Little Simon, the battery drummer, took up the mournful, urgent chorus. The soldiers scurried in confusion. Some froze in terror as a mouse might in the gaze of a snake. The breakfast cookfires were still smoldering, the pots and pans suddenly forgot, bedrolls discarded into heaps on the damp field.

"*Get* those *trails* down!" As one, the six six-pounder brass howitzers, two of which had been hitched and four had been *about* to, dropped to the meadow floor and turned south in a rough line. "*Canister!*" Dent yelled at his men, quickly planning his first-ever real battle. The target seemed to grow, with more rebels spilling out of the woods every moment.

"*Canister,*" the men chorused back, just as he'd taught them in countless days of gun drills.

"*Elevation zero!*" "*Elevation zero…*"

Men rushed forward with the powder charges, as others prepared the thin metal containers of musket balls.

"Charges…*ram*! Canister…*ram*!" Dent shouted, watching his men. From the corner of his eye, the infantry on his left opened fire with a sharp crack.

"Caps...*on! Clear* the guns...*Center* section: *FIRE!*" An earth-shattering roar rent the still air as Dent recalled, dimly, hearing the same command from the rebel line. Turning to see, a cloud of smoke billowed from the Rebels' direction as *their* volley was delivered. "*Stop vents and reload canister-on-ball!*" Dent shouted, and still, his men chorused back as he chanted, "If I *wasn't* a *gunner,* I *wouldn't* be *here...Left* section: *FIRE!*"

As Dent heard the whizzing of the rebel volley, he saw the gristly paths his guns made in the rebel line, as if a scythe had smacked down shocks of bleeding, shrieking, writhing wheat. "*Stop* vents and *reload canister-on-ball.* If I *wasn't* a *gunner,* I *wouldn't* be *here...Right* section: FIRE! *Stop* vents and *reload canister-on-ball!*" Dent yelled, turning back to his guns, but he was not *quite* prepared for the sight of some of *his* men lying on the grass, one not moving, others screaming from wounds. "*Quick* boys, they'll not return anything like *that* soon." *Too many of 'em, too close. Need to move the guns.* "Point at a *tree,* boys! *BATTERY! FIRE!*" Dent screamed, and six guns barked. He turned again to see the effect. He was both stunned and gratified to see that the splintered trees had amplified the power of the cannons, turning another grey-clad rank into a lifeless heap.

"Center section, get *your* guns up to the trees behind us! Trains, take the *forge wagon* with them! Hurry lads! Left and right sections: *Load double-canister!*" He glanced at Arbor, his shoulder and head bleeding, waving his grandfather's saber, pointing where the forge wagon was to go, still in his shirtsleeves. "*Left* Section: *FIRE! Limber and retreat.* Find the center and set up with good supports. We'll be right behind you." Again Dent turned, and now, through a growing pall of thick smoke, he could see the mounting confusion in the grey line. Loads of musket balls were tearing great rents into the otherwise orderly formations, building a gristly carpet on the field. He turned again and saw the infantry to the left, shrouded in smoke, lances of red flame still coming out, and another great cloud lanced red opposite *them.* Some blue suits, though, were making for the trees behind them.

Lieutenant Williams stumbled towards him in confusion, mumbling. "Sergeant, the men should be at Sunday services by now. Why are they still at gun drill? Have they eaten yet? What *is* that great *noise,* Sergeant? I smell powder. Oh my God, what is *that? Those* men are running away? Put them on *report...*"

"*SIR,*" Dent shouted, grabbing the officer by the shoulders, shaking him gently. "Sir," he said, as if to a child. "Two gun sections and the trains have moved to the woodline north of us," Dent said in his best parade ground manner. "You should be directing them in preparing the battery's next position."

Williams stared at him as if he hadn't heard, then suddenly, reality and recognition came, like an epiphany. "Yes," Williams nodded. "You're *right,*

Sergeant. I shall join the battery in the rear. Take charge *here*, if you would, and join us as soon as possible."

"Yessir," Dent said. There was a great noise behind him, and Dent turned to see a Rebel battery pointing at him no more than a hundred yards away. He threw himself to the ground when the smoke erupted from the bronze maws of two cannons, and everything went black.

● ● ●

When Dent awoke, it seemed dark and damp, with the smell of mist and smoke. He heard gunfire in the distance, somewhere. He raised his head, and a stab of pain lanced his head and neck. He laid it back down and waited for the pain to subside. Gingerly he brought his hand to his face, felt around to the side of his head. Stiff crusted blood covered the side of his head and neck, a large crease above his left ear. *Can't be that bad*, Dent thought *if I can still move my hand, even think.*

His vision cleared after a time, and he realized it wasn't dark after all; an ocean of smoke trapped in the trees was blocking the sun. Scattered sunlight filtered through the sulfurous clouds, lighting a ghastly tableau in the clearing. He pushed himself into a sitting position and looked around. He saw bodies that dotted the ground in the tangle of brush and grass of the meadow, scattered with muskets, tools, bedrolls, and clothing. Remnants of cookfires still smoldered, a coffee pot boiled, forgotten. A broken limber lay abandoned near the edge of the clearing, axle snapped off at the trail. A lame horse grazed dumbly nearby, saddle under its belly and a boot stuck in a stirrup. Two of his precious guns lay abandoned, surrounded by blue and grey-clad bodies. One had its wheels smashed, another's trail was broken. Nearby lay heaps of battery horses, their harnesses still fixed upon them.

The crash of musketry and artillery got louder and louder by the moment until he thought the battle was returning to the clearing. He laid back down for many moments, but no one showed themselves. *Only my ears getting unplugged from the noise.*

"*Well*," Dent said aloud, just to see how well his voice might work. "No sense staying *here*. Might as well get a move on." With this resolve, he gathered up his strength and once again sat up. When he was half-erect, the stabbing pain changed to a dull throbbing. He felt vaguely ill. He reached for his canteen. Gone. He looked around for another. He saw one in the middle of the camp and started to walk for it. He hadn't walked a dozen paces before he saw the canteen was splintered. The sun beat down on him through the trees and smoke. He felt dizzy, dry. *Must find water…*

He stood in the clearing turning slowly around, wondering where to go. Around him, men were caught in the rictus of violent death, limbs severed and torn, bodies mangled, faces in a hundred expressions: fear, anger, peace, surprise, desperation, no expression at all, no *face* at all. When he saw that not *all* were dead, some of the men in blue serge and homespun still moved. Dent stopped by one Johnnie, whose eyes moved. His face was blank, lips parched. His hands gripped a musket; his feet were nowhere to be found. He smiled thinly at Dent, closed his eyes, and died. *Boy just waited to see someone before he went to his Deliverance, just not wantin' to die alone.*

How long have I been here, and what time of day can this be? He looked up at the sky for the sun, orienting himself to what he took for the north. With the assurance of a Regular, he guessed it was still morning. The din of distant battle was overbearing, beating violently on Dent's aching head, but his need for water had not been fulfilled. Heedless that it might lead to the fighting, Dent picked up a broken musket with a fixed bayonet and started towards the trail that led north out of the clearing. *Here are some broken muskets, there a pistol, and over there a bent sword. Other than a few empty cartridge boxes, there's nothing that works. Very queer.* He searched in vain for a canteen or water bottle, prodding some of the still forms without results.

"*You* there," a voice called. Dent looked around. "I say *you* there! Sergeant! Over here!" A Major sat leaning against a tree, some ten paces off the trail, his right leg tied up in a splint. "What's your name and unit, Sergeant," he demanded brusquely.

"Dent, sir, Arbor's Battery of the Indiana Artillery...."

"*Where's* your battery, Sergeant?" The Major seemed impatient and slightly panicked. There was mild fear in the voice that tried to be authoritarian. *He's a Volunteer, perhaps a city councilman or some such.*

"Can't say as I *know*, sir. I got hit in the head," he touched the side of his face, "and I just woke up a few moments ago."

"Well, then, help me up, Sergeant. I have to get to headquarters and make my report."

"Yessir," Dent replied, picking the officer up by the shoulders while his head throbbed. "Which *way*, sir?"

"Same way you were going; up the trail north. Let me look at that head," the Major said. He peered at it with some distaste. "Hmm. Not that bad. Lucky for *you*, you have got a thick skull. Let's go."

"I was looking for water, sir..."

"Good, then we're on the right way. There's a creek about a half-mile north, runs right by a peach orchard..."

• • •

It was raining and dark when Dent woke up again. He didn't know *where* he was, or *how* he got there, or what *time* it was. All he knew for sure was that his head hurt like someone was beating on it. And it was raining.

Between the time he helped the Major up and the time he awoke again, he

13

was aware of a great number of things that happened, but they were a confused jumble of images and impressions. He recalled organizing crews for a James rifle and a six-pounder from a pair of artillerymen and a scattering of infantry. He had the particular image he had of blowing the cheeks off a gun carriage when the team was shot down in their traces. Then there was something about clubbing a couple of rebels with a wheel spoke and (or was that while?) defending a stand of colors. And there was a vivid image he had reloading some muskets while seeking cover in a little shed while the balls made splinters that showered down on him. He had a clear vision of locking arms with other sergeants and corporals as a bayonet charge surged forward into a clearing with a pond. And the last, most confusing, was when he was organizing the emplacement of a section of Napoleons in view of a pair of monstrous siege guns. He tried to open his eyes more than a slit, but a bright light in the corner of one eye stopped him. The stabbing pain from the light made him cry out.

"So, you're awake, then," a voice boomed in the darkness. *Queer. I should know that voice, but I can't place it.*

"Head," Dent moaned. "My head..."

"Quite a knock you've got there, me lad," the voice boomed again, this time a little quieter, the rain a bit louder. "Bleedin' for *fair* when we got here, you was. But the blood's stopped now. Nothing more left for your day's troubles than a goose egg on the noggin."

Dent rolled on his side and pried one eye open, forcing it to stay. He couldn't see the source of the voice, but he could see other wounded men. Most were lying down, many were sitting up. All had the ashen faces of badly hurt, frightened men who had used up what there was of them to use, and now they were hurt besides. They looked as if they had nothing more to give. Small fires kindled all around. And the rain pelted down.

"Where *is* this place," Dent demanded, in his best drill-field voice. "Who *are* you?" He was suddenly afraid he'd been captured, or worse, left behind in a retreat. Given the surprise of the morning, neither would surprise him at that moment, but it did make him a little sick.

"Me? I'm no one, in particular, goin' nowhere, doin' nothin' when I get there. Just waitin' here for Johnny Reb to come to gather me up with the rest of this rabble here. Nothin' left to this gang, I'll tell you, not after today. Nothin' left. That or the good Lord will come and take me home, or the Devil. Don't matter which now..."

Dent started, forcing himself to sit up even though his head rang near to bursting with the effort. He looked around him to see the source of the voice: a huge red-haired man wrapped in a gum blanket, his head lolling to one side and then the other with regularity. The legs of his pants were empty. "Don't hardly matter now, boy, don't matter now."

It HAS to matter. "*Got* to matter," Dent muttered to the dying man. "You just hold on here," he told him, as if issuing an order. "Hold this position until I find reinforcements." There was something that possessed him at that moment, something familiar that he'd known well, that he'd seen in others too, from time to time...

Years before, his father showed him the letter of appointment to the Military Academy at West Point, an appointment not easy to get for the son of a career NCO with no family. The post commander, a bellicose Major from South Carolina, shook him by the hand and gave him *sotto voce* advice about the great Academy on the Hudson. The fort garrison passed him in review.

But as he watched the marching men, he noticed something that unsettled him. The officers shouted orders, and the men obeyed. The sergeants shouted curses, and the men listened. The officers milled around the reviewing stand with the handful of ladies at the post while the sergeants and corporals brought the ponderous formation around, changing front, making a blue-coated mob into a disciplined unit, marking every drum beat with a footfall. The officers reported fawningly to the Major, passing on only what the sergeants told them. The sergeants watched the line, propped up the stragglers, pulled aside the faint.

Dent had headed for New York and the Plain on the Hudson in the spring of his eighteenth year but stopped at St. Louis, where he joined the artillery as a private. He was in Kansas in a week and was promoted to corporal in a month. He wrote his folks that he was all right, but he just couldn't see himself as an officer. He felt he owed it to the men who carved his toy muskets, taught him the long roll of the drum, showed him close-order drill, and how to saddle a horse—in short, how to *soldier*. He received a terse note from his mother in return, saying how disappointed his father was. A few days later, he got a telegram from his father. "Do your duty," was all it said.

That had been in 1859. Dent started fighting bushwhackers and free-soilers nearly two years before Ft. Sumter was shelled. In May, he was no longer a corporal in the Regular artillery; he was a Sergeant. He followed Lieutenant Lassiter (USMA, class of 1860) from one volunteer battery after another in Missouri, Iowa, Illinois, Wisconsin, and Indiana. There was no time to think of much more than the endless strings of green recruits fumbling with charge bags and rammers, choking horses with their rigs.

Now Dent found himself in pelting rain with a throbbing head and no idea where his unit was...or a *good* idea where *he* was. But he knew there were soldiers here who needed sergeants. There were probably plenty among them wearing the stripes, but they had either forgotten or had never known what they were *supposed* to do. They had been elected because they could read or knew their right from their left, or because they won some contest of strength. But they were never told what they were supposed to do.

Dent got to his feet slowly, measuring the pain in his head. *Not unlivable. I can do my duty.* There was a muddy track between buildings, lines with milling men, frightened civilians, and not a few children. The road, Dent could see, came up between two bluffs—the access to the river. He could see, further down the draw, the river and hundreds of men near it, in it, waving and crying at men disembarking from steamers. Lost, lost, they were saying, we're all lost. Take us away, they were saying. Sparks rose from smokestacks in the dark rain as steamboats came and went. As he descended, others were marching off steamboats and up the draw, bayonets fixed and leveled at the mobs who stood in their way.

Watching the men milling around without purpose, without weapons, hatless, soaked to the skin, cold, hungry, frightened, and miserable, Dent knew what he had to do. "Just turn on around," one of the skulkers called. "Get back on that there boat and go on home. This here war's all done." "Grant's drunk in the rear somewhere," another yelled. "Sure wish *I* was." "Best skedaddle afore the Rebs do it for ye. Nothin' here but graves."

And beaten *this* mob *was*, most farther from home than they had ever *been*, and in their *first battle,* they had seen good men die at their breakfasts. Not a few were smeared with powder from biting cartridges, with cracked lips and reddened eyes. *They had fought, many of them anyway. But for right now, they are done.*

Officers shouted, pleaded down by the river, and swore at the skulkers, who ignored them, or regarded them a curiously as they might a talking hare. A chaplain exhorted them with challenges to their faith and allusions to Daniel and the lion's den. "Not what they need," Dent muttered. "They need to remember *what* they are and *what* they're *here* for." As he staggered down the ravine, he found a frightened-looking corporal standing alone under a tree, face nearly black with powder grime and gripping his musket so hard his knuckles were white—still a soldier but needing direction.

"Corporal," Dent snapped. The young man jumped almost straight up. "Where's your section?"

"I...I...I don't....don't quite...." the boy stammered. His uniform was spattered with mud and red flecks, getting wetter by the moment. His face was grimy, and his voice cracked from thirst.

Good. Still willing but doesn't know how. "What's your name and regiment?"

"M...Michael...G...Garrison, C...Company E, fif...Fifteenth Iowa," the boy stammered, but the color was coming back to him.

"All right, then, come with me. *We* have work to do. We need to get your people back on the line. You want to do *that*, don't you?"

"Oh, yessir, I *do*. I do *indeed*." Down the gully, they marched, as up the same path came more and more men, bayonets lowered, fending off the army of stragglers as they came up from the landing. The skulkers were wild, frenzied in places, pleading, and exhorting the newcomers to just stop. Dent and Garrison ignored them; indeed, it seemed as if they were invisible to each other. Along the riverbank, Dent peered south, looking among the isolated individuals among the mobs. In a few moments, he found a burly sergeant sitting in the mud, alone, oblivious to his surroundings, already drenched and getting wetter. Dent squatted down beside him, watching his big moon-face in the flickering glow of a distant fire.

"Evening, sarge," Dent said quietly.

"Evenin' 'tis," he replied, not looking.

"Could you bear us a hand? We need to organize a fire. We were hoping *you* would."

The big face gazed at him passively, the eyes barely showing any recognition. "*What* d'ya be wantin' a *fire* for, then?"

"Grub," Dent replied, his voice still even. "The men need to eat."

A light appeared in the sergeant's eyes, and Dent almost started at the sight of it. "Aye, they need *that*, and a lot *else*." He looked away again and then down to the river. "And a few knocked *heads* if Kevin Murphy has *his* way." He looked at Dent again, almost as if seeing him for the first time, then he looked down at his massive, coarse hands, embarrassed. "And if you were to ask Kevin Murphy how in Perdition he got down *here*, he'll say that by all the saints he hasn't *any* idea, and he was just wonderin' that himself." Murphy stood up, a head taller than Dent. "A *cookfire*, is it?"

"Aye," Dent replied, pulling on his own brogue.

Murphy retrieved a battered bowler from somewhere in his coat and placed it on his sodden head at a jaunty angle. "Then, a cookfire we shall *have*." He looked around him thoughtfully, as if seeking old compatriots in a small crime. "And I'll get more fires a-burnin' just for dryin' out in this miserable *English* rain. You there!" Murphy shouted at a passing private. "Yes, *you*, Seamus! I don't bloody care *what* your name is, now *do* I, ya drunkard! Fetch us some firewood here, and find a keg of dry powder and be damned quick at it! And *you*, there! *Don't* take that innocent look with *me*, Seamus! Get your ass up the hill and get some kindling! *Shut* yer *pie-hole* and be quick on it, or I'll box yer ears fer ya! And *you*, ya goggle-eyed Paddy! I *don't* give a *damn* what...."

Dent left the fire organization in Murphy's capable fists and started up the gully. He walked with the stream of blue-clad reinforcements, who lowered their bayonets on the mobs as they marched through, four across. As he reached the top of the crest, he heard a dull booming down at the river. For a moment, the rough silhouette of a gunboat sat on the dark water and then vanished like an apparition. When he turned around, he saw Garrison standing by him. "Let's find something to *feed* them, Corporal," Dent said, hoping he sounded more convincing than he felt. *Where in hell am I going to find food for a hundred, leave alone a thousand or however the hell many there are down here...?*

Seeing a fire in the trees, he led off along a muddy trail off the main track. Soon they came to a large fire with a group of officers standing around it, warming themselves under rough canvas awnings. *Where there are officers, there's food.* "Beggin' your pardon, sirs, but I wonder where I might find some hot food for some of the men..."

"*What* men," a tall, severe-looking Colonel snapped.

"Down by the river, sir. They've been...."

"Skulkers," the colonel sniffed. "We will spare nothing for cowards such as them."

"Hear, hear," another said, sipping deeply from a flask. "Run away at first sight of..."

"Excuse me, sirs," Dent said, a fit of anger rising in him. "They ran away when they had no other choice. Look here," he pulled Garrison into the light. "See his face? Bit off all the cartridges he could find until there was no more to be had. When did you start fighting, Corporal?"

"B....before sunup, sir. I...it was still dark when the lieutenant got killed, and then we ran out of cartridges and then..."

"See there? Fought till he couldn't no more..."

"Rubbish," the colonel snorted. "You probably *told* him that story." The colonel, his uniform impeccable, strode towards Garrison. "That musket's never been fired, I'll wager my eyes. Give me *that*, you yellow coward..."

"Wait." A voice called across the fire. "I *know* these men." A captain, spattered with mud and grime, came around the fire, his hat akimbo, streaks of rain running down his chin. "Yes," he said, giving Dent a sly look. "Remember him *well*. He organized a battery from four odd guns and a handful of infantry on the Hamburg road. You recall, Tom, where we started to draw that first line this morning?"

"I believe I remember the *place*, George, but...," another Colonel answered, appearing dubious.

"Oh, it was *him*, all right. And the *corporal* here. Stood like a rock out on that very same road, loading and firing as if on a drill field. The men rallied to him like moss to a river stone. It was all we could do to get him to keep from charging the Rebs when he ran out of cartridges. Never got your name, boy..."

"Garrison, sir, but I..."

"Tut, *tut*, lad. Let's not speak of it. Such worthies as these do not talk of heroism until after the fight's done, *do* they, lads?"

"Fighting's done for *this* army," another Major, clearly in wine, growled.

"That drunkard Grant had better either surrender us now or pack up for Cairo again. We're *whipped,* I say, *whipped.* Only a *fool* says otherwise."

"Hear, hear," the Major with a flask added, swigging again.

"Beggin' yer pardon, sirs," Dent said, raising his voice. "*This army* may be whipped," he paused, letting the emphasis sink in, "but by the *Eternal,* there are a few *thousand* men down by the bluffs that need a fighting chance to pull together again. They'll do a lot more with full bellies than they will with empty ones. And you *gentlemen* had better ask *them* before talking about surrendering or retreating."

"*What!*" the immaculate Colonel exploded. "You insolent little *swine!* I'll have you bucked and gagged by sunrise! Summon a provost! I'll swear out charges this very moment..."

"*What's* your name, Sergeant," a disembodied voice asked from over the fire. Though small and quiet, the voice evidently carried some weight, for all the others fell silent on hearing it.

"William Dent, sir, with Arbor's Battery of the Indiana..."

"*Dent,* you say? Hail from Kentucky, do you?"

"Nossir, New Mexico. My Paw's people came out from Kentucky, I understand."

"I see. My wife has people in Arizona." There was a long pause before the voice returned with conviction. "Give him what he wants, Major Black. Colonel Worthington, could you please ask Generals Sherman, Prentiss, Hurlbut, and McClernand to join me here?"

"Yes, if you *wish,*" the immaculate Colonel replied insolently, "I'll detail the Corporal here..."

"No, you will go *yourself,*" the voice answered curtly. "The corporal has his *own* duties to tend to."

"General Prentiss is a prisoner, sir," another voice called, "but General McClernand is with the great battery. Saw him there not an hour ago with Captain Arbor..."

"You *saw* Captain Arbor," Dent blurted, forgetting not only his place but his immediate job.

"Indeed, I did. He's got a nick out of his shoulder, but otherwise, he's as hale as ever."

"Then I'll have to report...," Dent started.

"That's all *right,* Sergeant," the quiet General said. "You do what you set out to do. Feed them and see if they won't rally."

"For my own knowledge, General," Dent said, his head reeling from being on his feet for so long, "should anyone ever ask, may I trouble you for your *name,* sir?"

The ring of officers around the fire parted, making way as a small figure in a muddy coat limped forward on a crude Army crutch. He squatted down to pick up a burning branch from the fire and brought it to the stub of a cigar. The firelight danced on a scruff of dark beard, a round face, and a stern brow with gentle eyes. "A *Regular*, aren't you," he said softly.

"Yessir, I *am*. Third Artillery. Might I know *your* name, sir?"

A corner of the General's mouth pricked up slightly. "*My* name is *Grant*," he replied simply. Some of the officers around the fire thought this was hugely amusing but were stifled when the General glanced about. One surreptitiously found a spot on his uniform that merited closer scrutiny. "Take *that* the cauldron *there*, Sergeant. And I'd admire knowing how the men respond."

"They'll respond, sir," Dent replied with some enthusiasm. "A man will do nearly anything with a hot meal in him. And it's not that they don't *want* to fight, sir," Dent went on, his head throbbing painfully, "but they were badly surprised this morning. When, if I may speak *plainly*, sir, they should *not* have been."

"Oh, you may *speak*, Sergeant," the General replied, looking around the fire pointedly, "since others here of *higher* rank have, this day, been *plainer still*." No word was said for a moment, as the clean-looking officers gathered around the fire looked guiltily into the flames. "But you think the men will still fight? Will they follow orders from their officers?"

"I *know* they will fight, sir," Dent replied with an assurance he wasn't confident he had. He knew his own men in Arbor's battery, and he knew the Regulars, but dare he speak for that mob under the bluffs? "But, with respect, sir, they'll do what they're told, but not because they're ordered to, sir. They'll do it because it's their *duty*. And because their sergeant *will*, like as not, tan their hides if they *don't*."

The general faded a grin. "I suppose you may be right, Sergeant. If *perhaps* we should listen more to our non-commissioned officers than we do to those who have commissions, we would do far better in our campaigns. What do the men say of *me*, Sergeant?"

"Don't rightly know for my own knowledge, sir," Dent admitted, discounting the derision he'd heard down at the bluffs. He'd heard many conflicting views on the Commanding General, the usual mixture of soldier's grumbling and hero-worship, but tried to keep his own consul in such things. "But if the General sticks by them, they'll stick by the General, if the General doesn't mind my saying, sir."

"I do not mind at *all*, Sergeant. Send the Corporal back in a quarter-hour, and there'll be another cauldron. I'll send word to Captain Arbor of your mission. Lieutenant Mears, gather some men from the escort and get this cauldron down to the bluffs. There'll be a *fire*, Sergeant?"

"Yessir," Garrison answered, startling Dent. "Should be *several* by the time we get back."

"That's fine. Gentlemen, you should repair to your duties. It has been a terrible day today, but we will whip them tomorrow. Now, if we can collect together three good brigades next to General Wallace when General Buell moves in the morning..."

"I'll go with you, Sergeant," the muddy Captain said as Dent turned away.

"Thank you, *no*, sir," Dent replied. "With respect, sir, this is *sergeant's* business. But there is something you *can* do, sir."

"Yes, of *course*," the Captain replied. "What can I do?"

"Well, for one thing, sir, there's, um...I don't..."

"Remember the Hamburg Road?" The Captain grinned. "No, you wouldn't, but God knows I'll never forget it. For an hour, I had a thousand men under my command from a score of different regiments, but by *thunder*, we fought as we'd been bonded in blood all our lives. And I did see a sergeant like yourself pull a four-gun battery together as if by magic, and I saw him fall with a bullet through his brain.

"But I know you've been at this battle all day, you and the Corporal both, and I know these *nincompoops* at staff haven't. I was a sergeant in Mexico with Scott. And there are times I wish I *hadn't* taken this commission." He looked into the darkness. "Tell you what I'll do. I'll find a sutler somewhere; get him to put up some tobacco...."

"*That* would be *fine*, sir," Dent replied, "But we'll need *officers* with commands to *go* to soon. Once the men eat they could fall into idleness again if they're not given somewhere to go."

"Ah, I see," the captain replied. "I should send them down by the bluffs....?"

"*Nossir*; right up here'll be *fine*. They see officers down there, and they'll turn mulish again. We'll send 'em up here as they get fed. And a surgeon would be needed, as many of them have hurts, real and imagined, that should be tended to..."

"Leave it to *me*, Sergeant."

The officers ordered; the sergeants guided and prodded and yelled and got the job done.

And *that's* how the grim business moves.

Into the Fire

Not all soldiers have worn uniforms, and not all allies have been human...

The beast was old and snorted and shuffled in the dusty earth, lowing. It looked around, but the herd was gone. It had been left to die…alone.

The hunter crouched low in the grass downwind from the beast, dragging his long throwing spear behind him. The hunter was tired, feverish, and cold as the sun fell. His clan had a sickness that the shaman could not cure. Sick or well, they had to have meat, or the old ones would die, and the young would not grow. He clenched his spears and drew his heavy skins tighter to his body. The hunter had no faith in the shaman. He *had* confidence in his spears and his knife.

The waterholes where the beasts and men drank had dried up in the long summer. The sloths had grazed all the bamboo and reeds of the swamp after even *those* brackish water sources became parched. The sloths died with bellies bloated from lack of water. The clan had slaughtered them, but *that* meat was gone.

A missed throw would make the beast run, and the hunter was too sick to go far after it. He edged closer and heard a rustling in the dry grass nearby. He stopped and stayed still. A lion or bear may have seen the beast. A lion with flashing teeth and slashing claws could carry the hunter in her mouth; a bear could kill him with one blow. But the dip in the grass was too small for a lion or a bear. If it was not a lion or bear, the hunter was not concerned. Any *other* animals he could fight. He edged closer to the beast that listened to the wind, shaking its head. It grunted and snuffed, then started walking away from the hunter. *Don't run*, the hunter thought, prayed. *Don't run.*

The throw was far, but the hunter was desperate. He stood up quickly in the grass, aimed, and threw his long spear. The bone head glinted in the afternoon sun as it rose, and again as it fell before it struck in the small of the animal's back. The beast bolted and broke the spear, but the head was still buried in its thick hide. *It could get away!*

Suddenly, two dark shapes darted from the dip and pursued. *Strange. Not wolves or jackals, but like them.* The *not*-wolves were swift and caught up to the prey quickly. One *not*-wolf grabbed one of the beast's back legs; the beast spun around, throwing it off. The other got to the throat and tore it open. Blood spattered on the dusty ground. The beast lowed loudly as blood gurgled into its throat. A swinging horn found a *not*-wolf's chest.

The enraged quarry stomped the wounded *not*-wolf in defiance, lowing in a fury. The other *not*-wolf snarled and barked, snapping and dashing at the prey. The hunter gripped his stabbing spear with both hands as he ran and circled behind the beast, dashed forward, and thrust down quickly between its shoulder blades. It lowed once more, fell to its knees, and was still.

Hunter and *not*-wolf stood over the beast, panting in the cold with the sweet smell of fresh-kill blood in their noses. They looked at each other: two hunters, successful together. The hunter released the thrusting spear and pulled out his obsidian knife, polished to a dull black sheen after generations of use. The hunter gutted the carcass and examined the liver. He could see no lesions that showed evil spirits, nor could he smell poisons in the dark brown mass. He quickly cut open the chest, reached inside to dislodge the spear point, and removed the heart.

I eat the heart of the kill that I may share its strength and courage.

He finished the prayer and bit into the muscle. Salty blood washed down his throat. The *not*-wolf crept up to the carcass, sniffing tentatively. The animal sniffed and nuzzled his dead kin and looked up at the hunter. The hunter cut off a small piece of the heart and threw it to the *not*-wolf.

He opened the stomach and dumped out the contents to make a pouch for the liver. He quickly gutted the *not*-wolf and examined the liver as he had the other beast. It was nearly dark by the time he was done.

The *not*-wolf gobbled down the lungs of the beast and of his fellow *not*-wolf and followed the hunter at a distance as he dragged the kills to a spur of rocks. It would be colder soon. In winter, the grassy sea was deathly cold at night. As the hunter gathered wood, the *not*-wolf sat by the carcasses, watching. The hunter struck the stones to summon the sacred spark, chanting to the fire and grass gods, blowing the sacred breaths into the golden embers the gods made. Grass warmed and flared as the flame spread, warming the small sticks. The gods had smiled on the hunter again.

The hunter cut a haunch from the beast with his knife and impaled it on a sharp stick. As the meat sizzled over the fire, he tended to his spear points and made a new shaft for his throwing spear. On the handle of his stout killing spear, he carved a small image of the beast and the *not*-wolf in their death battle, imagining the story he would tell his clan.

When the meat was well blackened, the hunter started to eat it. The *not*-wolf crept to the fire and sat, watching. The hunter cut off a chunk and threw it down. The animal ate. Another *not*-wolf appeared out of the shadows—a female, heavy with pup. The hunter cut another piece and threw it to her. The hunter wrapped himself in his skins and slept; the *not*-wolves crouched by the fire…and slept,

The hunter awoke to growling and howling and barking. He pushed the pile of dry grass and twigs he had prepared into the embers of the fire. The fire flared with the new fuel, lighting the *not*-wolves and a bear, taller than the hunter, making for the carcasses. The *not*-wolves snarled and barked, darting at the bear with snapping jaws and pinned-back ears, tails wrapped between back legs. The bear roared and swatted at the faster animals.

The hunter took up a burning stick and ran at the bear. The bear, not accustomed to fire, roared in confusion and rage. The man thrust the torch at the bear that swatted at him with claws as long as a finger. A *not*-wolf lunged at the bear and bit into tight skin. The bear shook the animal off, roared once again in defiance, turned, and ran away into the dark.

The hunter scarcely believed it. *I am the mightiest of hunters! I have beaten a bear alone. No, not alone...* The *not*-wolves huddled near him, one injured by a claw. The hunter picked up the wounded animal and went to the fire. He made a salve of ashes and spit and applied it to the wound.

After dawn, he built a litter drag for the carcasses and started for his clan cave. The *not*-wolves followed him, the wounded one limping bravely. When he arrived home, the clan celebrated the hunter's return. They carved up the carcasses and scraped the skins. They sliced the livers into strips and dried it over the fire. The skulls were smashed and the easily-digested brains for the children, the sick, and the old ones. Buts and cartilage were split and twisted and spread out in the sun; bones scraped and doused in brackish water.

The *not*-wolves watched from outside the cave. The clan eyed them suspiciously. The hunter fed them from his portion. The shaman called them evil spirits. The hunter told his saga of the fight with the beast and the bear, the *not*-wolf that gave its life for the hunter and his fellows. The clan looked at them again with fear. The hunter fed them from his hand.

"They followed me, they watched over me, and I fed them," he told them. "Soon, the female will bear pups that will be our servants. We will call them *the beasts that follow*," the hunter declared.

Now, we call them dogs.

The Charge

Errol Flynn made this sort of thing look as easy as a fox hunt and as clean as a morning ride. Too easy, and much too clean...

They wait.

Officers, adjutants, aides, and couriers at the top of the rise, watching; the squadrons mass just behind the hill, listening. The horses snort and snuff, shake their heads at acrid wisps of smoke wafting on the wind. The men steady the beasts with caresses and soothing words. Flags and guidons roll and snap lazily in the breeze.

The Cavalry Reserve has moved three times this day, from early morning on the green near the tavern to mid-morning near the little church and graveyard, to midday here, behind the long ridge. The boom of cannon and crack of muskets mark the battle between infantry and guns, skirmishers, and screens. A stray cannonball bounces over the hills ricocheting off the firm ground, and rolls, smoldering, to a stop…innocent and spent.

Couriers race to-and-fro; officers, watching the battle in the valley, their mounts frothing, passed letters, maps, orders. His Lordship's compliments to the Officer Commanding the Cavalry Reserve. The enemy is expected to break on the right flank. The Officer Commanding is asked to act accordingly and pursue, supplementing the main army's advance by cutting off the enemy center's retreat.

Very well, the Officer Commanding accepts and will comply with his Lordship's request. *Instructions* are muttered by the Officer Commanding; colonels *ask the favor* of majors; majors *suggest* to captains; captains *instruct* lieutenants; lieutenants *order* sergeants; sergeants *threaten* men. Scouts take out at a gallop.

Splice the main brace.

The cooks break out the watery rum, gin, and wine. The men grumble at it. Corporals shout at privates to take their rations or be damned. They share their tots with brief salutes. The light infantry nearby curse the horsemen; the horse gunners curse their burdens; the cavalry curse all but each other.

It shall be soon, after all the marching and riding: the breeze shifts, the stench of the fight in the valley and woods stronger than ever.

The smiths and farriers finish their work, the harness-makers help them to load the forge-wagons and workshop carts. The musicians and surgeons quietly discuss their duties. The chaplains say prayers. The men pray. The horses scuff the ground…and, smelling powder and blood on the wind, perhaps *they* pray.

Bugles flourish—drums rattle. Men mount; packs on; fall in. An orgy of restrained, nervous, trained, instinctive, frenzied movement and the body becomes a unit, lined up on the dirt track called a road in these parts. NCOs curse their slovenly soldiers: horses bray and snort, stagger and rear.

They line up on the road as if for a parade, cuirassiers and dragoons, hussars and lancers, light foot and horse artillery. Baggage and shop wagons hastily move to the rear. Surgeons don aprons. Musicians roll litters, drums, and bandages. Pipes and fifes trill through the noise.

COLUMNS of four, BY the right, TURN! BATTERY order! MARCH!

Infantry drums beat, cavalry bugles blare. Horses and men move up the slope to the ridge top, across and down into the valley, to the battle, to the enemy. Those ahead raise clinging dust that packs the sinus, coats green and blue uniforms, scarlet and yellow, black and gold. The men strike up simple songs of marching and hardship. The sound of the battle grows.

They glimpse the battle in the distance as they top the rise. What had been marked by sound and smell for most of the day grows form, shape. His Lordship's infantry is pushing into the woods with the enemy falling back before them. Tentative ribbons and spots of panic can be seen on the far ridgeline to the right, on the other side of the valley.

A farm is on fire in the middle of the valley. Dots and piles of bodies and wreckage strewn about the blazing barn and demolished cottage as if cast away by a willful child, toys broken and no longer amusing. The guns grow louder. The woods are dense with smoke. A battery rides up hastily, gunners rush to serve their piece, touch off the howitzer before the horses are away. The horses bolt, grooms run after. The cavalry rides in parade-ground order down the road, one squadron after the other alongside the battlefield, around the woods, up a small knoll splitting the valley into two shallow bowls. Soldiers huddle along the knoll, exhausted, decimated, dirty, and wracked with pain and sickness from smoke, fear, and battle. They stare at the clean men and horses, disbelieving, spiteful.

A vidette, his tiny pony nearly ridden dead, scuffles to the head of the column. They are *there*, he points, and they are *over there*, down that track and along the edge of the wood. They are in disorder and are retreating on the right, yes, but their *center* falls back well. No, I must find his Lordship and make a full report. No, I pray, sir, I cannot stay—good hunting to you.

A small party of hussars is detached to make a reconnaissance, find, fix, and report back. Dragoons dismount and deploy on foot, unsling muskets, their horse-holders behind a copse. Lancers and cuirassiers dismount, adjust bridles, and cinches. The light-foot battalions catch up to the horsemen, deploy alongside the dragoons. Horse guns follow, rattle and clatter.

In moments a hussar rides back. *Found them*, he shouts. *Up and at them*, the order is passed. The column again snaps up smartly, breastplates gleam in the half-sun, lance pennons lazy, hussar helmets sway down the road.

A dispatch rider rushes forward, new orders. His center has withdrawn more swiftly than hoped. You are at the flank of his *center*, not his *right*. Careful you do not overreach.

Before them, the enemy. Ahead is another road crossing the valley, protected here and there by trees and thickets, stone fences, and walls. He retreats down that road. Scattered along the road, exhausted remnants of his army guards the refugees of shattered units and baggage wagons, duels with his Lordship's skirmishers from the center, with hussars from the Cavalry Reserve. Small bands of his horsemen form jagged lines, wait.

Form line.

They haven't enough infantry for square, not here, the officers decide. His horse cannot countercharge, not nearly enough to matter. There is room behind for us to regroup if we avoid the obstacles. Inform the rear we have found him and to hurry or miss the fight.

They form a wide line, four horsemen deep, quickly. The horses smell fear. They prance, shiver, twitch ears.

Forward at the walk.

Their line is as long as the road through the valley. Lancers strip pennons; dragoons check muskets; hussars wave and flex sabers; cuirassiers charge pistols; musicians move back. Colors in the center, guidons at the flanks.

The enemy sees them, and there seems to be some panic. Stay in the *ranks*; you go when you're *told*. You'll die on my order and not before, laggard.

Trot.

Cannon line up before a wall, their officers shouting in their frightening foreign tongue, horses white-flecked with foam. The cavalry's long gleaming line is approaching...

Gallop.

Horses move faster, knees grip flanks, leather slaps, gauntleted hands twist bridles for better grips. The long lines become ragged, bend around the slightest contour of ground. Cannons boom before them, the balls whistle and sigh through the ranks, bowl over an occasional horseman.

Gunners reload with iron scrap from the forge floors, sponges smoldering, powder measures cast aside. Infantry wheels. *Form square! M*ore guns draw up. *Hurry lads before they...*

CHARGE!

Spurs to flanks... *break through here and the day is ours*... sabers point...

form square... lances crouch... *steady on, boys...* pistols draw and cock... *hold here, or we are undone...* reins in teeth... *unlimber that gun...* chests down on horse's necks... *hold your fire...* swords slap flanks... *mark your targets...* froth blooms... *aim low boys... on them before they...*

FIRE!

Massed muskets erupt in sheets of flame and smoke... *they are upon us...* saddles empty... *kneel down...* pistols crack... *up boys...* horses fall... *reload...* men scream... *now lads...* sabers flash... *here they come...* infantry volley... *form four ranks...* clubbed muskets swing... *with the bayonet...* guns roar... *hold them lads...* grapeshot shrills... *oh God where is everyone...* lances strike home... *they are through...* horses shy... *sound recall...* wool burns... *give them canister...* horse guns blast at infantry squares... *I am dead sir...* cold steel cleaves flesh... *hit them again boys...* screaming iron sears bone... *we are lost...* flailing hooves meet bayonet walls... *back here you motherless cowards...* a ball passes through horse and rider... *rally here I say...* horses screech in panic... *infinite mercy have pity on us...* light infantry thunders into the fray... *oh I am shot...* muskets crash... *have we won sir... have we won...?*

Now the valley is still, fields and trees shrouded in mist and smoke. The battle continues, rattles and roars dimly, somewhere else. The dead and dying horses and men—friend and foe together—form a ghastly carpet on the valley floor. Dragoons chase away scavenger birds, villagers, and dogs; kick away rooting pigs. Chaplains with lanterns give water and comfort to the dying, blessings to the dead. Musicians carry away to the surgeons—their aprons already black with blood—those that may live.

A cuirassier, back broken, screams for relief. A hussar nearby, both legs crushed, obliges his mate with a pistol, then dies himself.

Is our battle won? Someone asks. A young officer, quite ill, streaked with dust, mud and blood, powder and foam, dispatches another lame animal with the stab of a shattered lance.

What *battle*, he wonders. I do not *know* battle. I only see *this horror. This cannot* be the battle that I have waited for all my life.

Battle is glory, or so I was told...

Family Business

In the aftermath of a tragedy, we go on...

Captain Henry Potter stood over the catwalk that straddled *California*'s engine room, watching the divers as they came up with the foot-long mounting bolts. The engines had to come out of old *California*, still sitting in the Pearl Harbor mud. Her sister ship, *Tennessee,* needed engine parts. *California* would get new engines.

"Captain Potter," the loudhailer called down. "*Ensign* Potter reporting at the companionway forward." *A pretty common name*, Potter thought. Puzzled, Potter struggled out of his coveralls, straightened his khakis, and climbed up the ladders to the main deck, making his way forward. Since he'd taken over command of this particular Pearl Harbor victim half a year before, Potter had removed all her surviving guns and serviceable equipment. The bombs that sank her had mostly affected the hull below the waterline and aft of the main funnels, letting her settle on an even keel. She would be rebuilt as practically a new ship and had little need for her old machinery or armaments.

Just forward of the A-turret ring stood a young man in an ill-fitting uniform. *Another gangling boy put into uniform for no other reason other than he passed some tests.*

"Sir," a familiar voice called added. Potter regarded the ensign thoughtfully. *This* young man was *not* a stranger. On either side of where they stood, sparks flew from workers grinding weld nuggets. An air hammer someplace below reverberated in the cavernous hull.

"Well, *hello*, Ernie," he called out, extending his hand. "What in hell brings *you* here so soon? You haven't finished your junior year."

"No, sir," the boy replied as they shook hands. "They offered some of us Reserve commissions *this* year if we'd go into specialized fields. I'm tired of school, anyway." He looked out at the busy harbor. The old Battleship Row was aswarm with small boats and tenders. Several tugs pulled at the overturned hulk of Oklahoma while two others blasted water into the muck beneath her, trying to pull her free.

"Oh," Potter said, relieved. Some infractions of Navy regulations could win an ROTC cadet less-choice billets, but there were few ways a young man could get an early commission. "I thought...well, never mind *what* I thought," he exclaimed. "Good to see you. *How's* your mother? Have you heard from Jane? Your Uncle Frank wrote to say Bobby joined the Army Air Corps. What about...?"

"Oh, *Mom's* fine," the ensign interrupted. "Sends her best." He was quiet. "*Still* wants to come out," he muttered. Potter winced. He remembered the telegram he received, not three hours after the radio announced the Japanese attack, sending him direct to Pearl. After Midway, it seemed safe to allow civilians back to Hawaii, *but...*

"I *can't* have her out here. You know, the Japs still fly over once a month or so." the captain sighed, "but that's not official, so you *didn't* hear it from *me*." The older man stared across the platform at Ford Island, watching the hive of activity at the temporary workshops that studded the low, sandy rock. Trucks hauling scrap to the inland pits rose dust on the unimproved trails.

"It's *OK*, Dad. I understand. And Mom will, too. Someday. Anyway, Jane's joined the Red Cross, apparently," the boy went on. "At least that's what it *looks* like. I talked to Bobby just before he got on the train. Said he would take some officer's course and be an Air Corps Captain in a few weeks because he's got so many flying hours. Uncle Frank got a letter from somebody...dunno who...said they'd make him a Major if he'd come back into the Army to instruct pilots. He said he'd think about it..."

"Huh," the elder Potter muttered, remembering that his older brother had been a pilot in the last war but never left the 'States. He had always resented missing the action. "When'd *you* get into town?"

"Last night. I spent hours getting my orders straightened out, then wrangled a billet at the Lanikai Hotel. The personnel guys told me to look up my new CO...um, sir."

"Oh, well. But...*what?*" Potter stared at his son, bewildered. "What was that last bit, you said? Your *new* CO?"

"Well, yes, sir. See, *that* was one of the specialties that they offered: salvage engineering. I'm to be on one of the new seagoing salvage tugs, *Apache*, she's called. I'm to be the assistant salvage officer. I'm to train under you until she comes out from Bremerton."

The captain blinked as if he'd been stunned by a flashbulb. After a deep sigh, "do you know how I got *into* this job," he said finally. "When I graduated from the Academy, I got drunk and piled up my car..."

"I *know*, Dad. You've told us a *hundred* times..." A loudhailer garbled something on *Maryland*, two ships down. "You were supposed to be a flier, but you hit your head..."

"But I *didn't* tell you the *other* half. It was *who* I piled into: my own skipper. His Academy classmate was in BuPers at the time. I swear he always had it *in* for me..."

"Yeah, Dad. You told me *that* when I turned the Academy down for Yale. Said, 'the Academy is the incubator of the Navy. ROTC is for dilettantes and hangers-on. But keep your nose clean,' you said..." A klaxon sounded across the island, followed by a muffled explosion and a fountain of water. "What was *that*?" Ernie asked, startled.

"If I had to guess," Potter said, clearing his throat, "the bomb disposal guys found something they couldn't move. Happens here a few times a week." He drew pensive, somewhat wistful. Slowly he turned around. "You *coming, Mister* Potter? You can meet the rest of the crew. Get your gear from the quartermaster before I show you the ship. A ship in salvage is the *dirtiest* place you can imagine, especially when all the waste tanks haven't been reached yet. As the newest officer aboard, you'll set the midnight watch. I'll have to redo the watch bill. We'll have dinner at the officer's club tomorrow night and introduce you formally to the mess. I *trust* you have whites ready..."

• • •

"Have you been to see George?" It had been nearly a week since his son joined his ship.

"No," Potter lied, "no, I haven't." He and three other salvage masters had been there, declared the hulk to be hopeless so resources could be spent on vessels that had a chance of fighting again. "You *want* to go?"

"Yes." The two officers went to a gangway on the harbor side. On the landing stage below, Potter looked around for a boat, motioning to a small landing craft-like torpedo lighter to come alongside. They stepped aboard.

"Take us to *Arizona*, boatswain." The boat surged gently ahead and then came about. On Ford Island across from *California*, beams of *Arizona's* superstructure were being cut for other patch jobs. Blown into several pieces, her hull couldn't even be raised for scrapping, but her superstructure had been cut off and taken to the scrap heaps.

"*Where*, sir," the boatswain asked.

"Anywhere along here," Potter motioned to the dark hull shape just below the water. The vessel puttered to a stop.

A destroyer churned through the channel towards the harbor mouth, patches of rusty steel still visible on her hull where it had been patched. Potter watched the sight with professional detachment. "Marcus *does* know his business," he muttered at length, turning to his son. "*That* vessel was cut to the waterline amidships; I called her a wreck but *Marcus*..." He stopped. Ernie had pulled a bible out of a jacket pocket. Sandwiched in the leaves was a small flower.

"The last of Mom's flowers from last year," Ernie said. "You know for a *fact* he was aboard? They never *found* his body."

31

"Yes, he was on engine watch. If he was where he was supposed to be, he wouldn't have had a chance." Potter stopped. "They offered to send me someplace else, but..."

"I know. Salvage skippers are always hard to find." Ernie picked up the flower. "George picked this the last time he was home; said Mom could give it back to him when he got back again." He dropped it into the oily water. "Sorry, Georgie; Mom couldn't come." In the smooth oily water, the flower seemed perched on the surface. Softly, the coxswain sang:

Day is done; gone the sun;
From the lake, from the fields, from the sky.
All is well; safely rest;
God is nigh.

Both officers looked at the petty officer. "That was *beautiful*, boatswain," Ernie said.

"Yes, lovely. Thank you."

The boatswain cleared his throat. "Not everyone knows 'Taps' has words." He paused. "Family, sir?"

"My would-have-been brother-in-law," Ernie said. "Known him all my life, like a brother. My *sister*..."

"Yes, sir, I understand. Forgive the intrusion."

"That's all right," Potter said, thinking of George, his Academy classmate's oldest son. He would have to tell the father—now on a destroyer somewhere on the Atlantic—about today. "Do *you* have family, boatswain?"

"Four brothers, sir. One's a policeman, one's out *here* somewhere with the Army, the other two too young. I joined the Navy when the Germans invaded Poland. Hard *not* to with a name like Wiersneiwski."

"I suppose so," Ernie said. "Take us back, please. *We* have a *ship* to repair."

Moles

For some, going to war is just like every other day, with a few extra hazards thrown in...

Jack dumped another handful of dirt into the sled behind him, working by feel. The carbide lamp on his hat guttered dimly, barely lighting the shaft face inches from his nose. He felt wet marl piled up to the rim of the sled. *Tap, tap* on the runners, and the sled pulled back.

Jack and the sled emerged into the tailings gallery after moving fifty yards backward through a mineshaft only as high as a man could stoop. He picked himself off the sled and shook some of the mud off him. His leather kneepads dug into his shins and thighs. The marl in the sled was unceremoniously dumped into a water-filled pit next to the hole. Pierce—the next miner—tied the sled pull-rope to his foot and crawled into the inky shaft.

The miners from the coal pits of Wales, the tin mines of Cornwall, and the iron ranges of Ontario dug shafts into the backs of hills that snaked across No-Man's Land to the German trench lines. When they had dug far enough, they built great rooms—galleries—that they packed with explosives and touched off. The generals hoped, and the soldiers prayed, that it would help the armies—stuck in trenches that ran from the North Sea to the Alps—gain more than a hundred yards for every thousand lives.

And *this* war was supposed to have been over a month after it started.

The tailings gallery smelled of old sweat, stagnant water and wet wool, of burned kerosene, and a little of mustard gas. It had kerosene light and better air, water for the miners, and tea and mush on good days.

Jack sat near the air pump bellows that wheezed to move air up a hundred feet and back over a mile. Two young boys, impressed for the job from a French mine, strained at the crank. Lanterns flickered in the shifting air of the back shaft. Jack took a pull on a water bottle and allowed some to wash down his muddy chin. He stared at the brown and black mud and shoring the gallery's timbers, too weary to think, too exhausted to rest.

The laterals that the miners struggled to dig on their knees were lower and narrower than regular mineshafts. The walls were weak, for they were long—in soft dirt, not rock. The air was terrible, and there was little of it, and only their hat lights pierced the darkness. Cave-ins were frequent.

But, the engineers reasoned, what would it matter how strong the laterals were when the intent was to destroy them when done? Aye, the miners answered, what *would* it matter...? Welshmen had been miners since the dawn of time, it seemed. Nor could anyone remember when there wasn't a pit somewhere in Wales being worked by generations of men and boys.

Jack studied the tailings-pile, how it had grown in the past days. Other men struggled to fill the larger trolleys going out of the gallery, removing the tailings that would have to be hidden from balloon-observers. He wondered how they were hiding it now, this different-colored stuff.

He rubbed his forehead against the pain, the dense air making a ringing in his ears. The sounds of dripping water and the wheezing air pump grated his nerves.

He dreamed, dimly, of his home, Grmndllity, a sooty village on the coast of Wales with a name that only the natives could pronounce correctly. But there, after fourteen hours of digging under the earth, at least his wife would be waiting for him. She may have been a toothless hag who snored like a saw, but she kept a good house, was a fair cook, had a sharp sense of humor, and was more comfort than a pile of straw in a drafty barn, cold mush and weak tea, and a chorus of Maxim guns with cannons for accompaniment in the night.

But the mines were a way out of the trenches with their hopeless waiting, enormous rats, and over-the-top charges into the Hun guns. There was a sense of order to swinging a pick in the dark. Swing back, catch the weight just at the top, snap and pull down, the shock of impact and wet *thut* into the earth that splintered into movable fragments, twist the pick and up again. It was regular, familiar, reassuring. Not at all like the other-world landscape of shell holes and trenches crisscrossing hill and field in a sea of mud and barbed wire, stinking of gas and the dead...

And this is what we do, Jack thought. *Me, my brothers, my father, and his father and his. And my uncles and my Ma's father and my wife's and...*

The trundle of the sled woke him from his reverie. Pierce was coming back. The winch creaked, the four men on the winding gear straining at the work. Pierce emerged with the tailings and rolled off the sled. Jack duck-walked to the shaft as the sled was dumped.

"What say, Pierce," Jack rasped, cracking a filthy grin.

"Loot of har" clay ahid, I'm thinkin,' Jocko. May need hammer and drill on't."

Jack winced inwardly. *That's a two-man job: one holding the drill and t'other swingin' the hammer. One miss and its two broke arms, fifty yards through a cold shaft and another mile to air. Blessed Sacraments...*

"An' I thinks I hear diggin' in thar," Pierce added under his breath, not looking at Jack.

Oh, no! Jesus and Mary, no. He'd heard of other mineshafts running into Hun countermines, of battlefronts a yard high and a yard across, fighting with pick and shovel and pistol... *Sweet Jesus, no! I've no wish to bash a fellow mole, even if 'e is a Hun...*

Jack tied the sled rope around his ankle and went into the shaft on his hands and knees. Every forward move brought pain, the heavy sled tugging his leg, hip, back, and groin. He splashed through shallow puddles about mid-shaft—under a shell-hole, probably—and clambered around a boulder just after. In a typical mine, they'd have drained the first and cracked the next, but not here. *Here we carve out a hundred yards every two days or...*

He stopped, straining at dull sounds. *Diggin,' but I thinks it our diggin.'* To the north, a Canadian battalion was digging another shaft for the same mine; to the south, an English one. *It's one of them.*

Jack's head ran softly into the shaft face, and he stopped to rest. He pulled the sled forward on its hard runners and felt around. *Ah, Pierce, ya gob. Cleaned up right lovely as always. Put us all to shame, ya will...*

Thunk!

That were too close and just the other side of the face. By the saints, I'll not be fightin' Huns in this hole...

Jack took his shovel and pick from the sled box, crawled behind the sled. He waited. The silence roared in his ears, tiny sprites of light dancing before him. He shook his head briefly, throwing off the illusion. Once before, in a cave-in, he'd had the same thing happen. Some of the other moles called it a rapture. *This must be what the grave would be like. On me soul, I'd as soon not get killed in this little...*

Thunk!

NO! Jack clutched his tools hard to his aching chest. *I'll not fight down here...*

Squirming into the sled, he *tap-tapped,* and the rope tightened. *At least I won't be in here when they...*

Baloom!

An avalanche of dirt and mud poured onto the sled, into Jack's face. Concussion blasted at his ears. Harsh electric light flooded the tunnel, and Teutonic voices shouted loudly. Jack lay still, eyes closed, buried under a thin layer of dirt and mud, barely breathing. Heavily-shod feet clomped into the shaft... two, three, four pairs crawled swiftly across him. The sound receded down the tunnel. *Got to warn 'em; can't let 'em get chopped like that.*

BOOMBOOMBOOMBOOM!CRASH!

The gun reports and the collapse of the tunnel rang in his ears, echoing and reverberating on the dank walls.

BOOMBOOM!

But that was outside, by God. Up above. There's a battle up there.

A blast of air blew through the tunnel as Jack struggled to his knees. Wiping the dirt and mud out of his eyes, he blinked. *Black. Pitch black. And no sound. Am I dead, then, and this is Purgatory? Will I feel cold in Hell?*

"*Hilfe*," a tiny voice called in the dark. "*Hilfe.*"

"I'm in Hell with a Hun, then," Jack muttered. "A Hun calling for help if I don't mistake it."

"*Hilfe.*"

"Hallo! Hallo!" Jack called. He felt around him. The mud walls were still there, a bit wider than before. He felt around for his tools without luck. *Where'd...?*

"*Hilfe.*"

Up tunnel. Up towards the Hun lines. A Hun got himself trapped in his own shaft. Well, the Devil wit' ye. I've troubles of me own. Hilfe yerself, ya gob.

Jack had been in cave-ins before. Most miners had by the time they got to their 'teens—great gouts of rock and dust, flashes of flame from exploding gas. The chest turns to lead as the air goes bad. Men go mad. He was in a shaft for three days once when he was not quite ten. Before the rescuers got there, a dozen men had died. Their big lungs just wanted too much...

Jack started to crawl back towards his own lines and got about five yards before his way was blocked. *Cave-in. Sealed me at the Hun end. Aw, the bloody Hell...*

He turned around and sat in the cold mud. Somewhere in the tunnel, water dripped. *We were near half across. There was no more than a day's dig to the next gallery. Fifty yards. But now? One way out. Towards the Huns.*

He crawled forward, his chest aching from the stale air. The pleas of "*hilfe*" got louder, briefly, then quieter again.

Jack remembered one cave-in he'd been outside of, moving rock and dirt and pumping water for four days and nights, and all the while, the *clang-clang* on the car rail told the rescuers that someone was still alive...

"*Hilfe...*"

Why in the Hell do we do this, then? Sweat and freeze in these holes? Coughing up our lungs before we see our wee ones grow tall. Watching the women march down to the mines whenever that lonesome whistle locks down, the whistle that means more men have died in the worthless pits. Women always clad in black for a husband or father or brother or uncle or son...

The mud was deep as he crawled. The air changed. Lime. Shale dust. More rock. *The Huns have been in rock, and we've been in clay. Small wonder we could hear them.* The water up to his elbows smelled of the poison gas and the unburied dead decomposing in No-Man's-Land.

As he crawled forward, the water rose to his chest. *I shall drown surely. No chance to dig out even if I go back for me tools. Too deep. The roof caved in somewhere, and now it's flooding. Ah, saints preserve me...*

Miners from his village went to France once. A train tunnel in the Alps got caved in. The pit owners had a stake in it and wanted it reopened. But the miners dug for their fellow moles, those they could still hear clanging on the rails and rocks all that while. They didn't know the Frenchmen a whit, but they knew miners...

He stopped. The air changed again. Clear. Fresh, open air. *Sweet God in Heaven be praised.* He crawled forward again. The sounds of battle were distinct but soft, far away. He crawled and stretched out a hand. The floor was gone. There was some light outside. A shell had blown a hole through the German tunnel just after the Huns breached Jack's shaft. *Whatever it was that trapped them Huns on our end, let me out on theirs. If that isn't a fine thing.*

Jack sat on the edge of a crater, looking up at the starlit sky. *Let's see, I went underground at half-past eight in, unloaded that last sled at a quarter of five. And now 'tis full night. Where did the time go, then? I must have been out some.*

"*Hilfe,*" a tiny voice called behind him. "*Hilfe.*"

And what of you, then, Hun? Was you born to these pits like I was? Not likely you were a society swell if you're down here. No, likely you're like me. Born to dig in the dark, if not for the mines and the owners then for other moles, for the widows up above, for the wee ones of your neighbors. Such as us were for these pits since Cain killed Abel.

"Aw, sweet *Jesus,*" Jack muttered, turning back into the dark hole, listening for the voice of his fellow miner, "Did ya *have* ta do *this* ta *me*? I'm *comin'*, brother Hun; I'm *comin'*."

Marbury Rose

On occasion, civilians step in when the military needs help...

Grace watched the dim dawn over the smoke-enshrouded coast. Small boats bobbed and wallowed around her in seas much too rough for them. *Marbury Rose*, her Uncle Edmund's 100-foot Thames yacht, led a long column of day-sailors, trawlers, coasters, and fishing smacks. Their job to pick the tattered British Army out of France and carry it home while the *Luftwaffe* tried to destroy the unarmed boats that had no business being there. The RAF occasionally swooped down to see the flotilla rolling in the angry Channel swells, doggedly making for the dark, forbidding Dunkirk shore.

This was the last battle of the Sea Fencibles, the *fishermen's militia* that the Navy so derided and yet depended on for sea-trained manpower since time out of mind.

Grace watched the fighter planes in their swirling, deadly dance overhead. It reminded her of circling scavenger birds. Occasionally a plane would explode, or a parachute would appear to break the illusion. It all seemed so unreal, with her Colin there in France, perhaps hurt, perhaps worse.

Closer to shore, the sea flattened, but there were worse hazards. A minesweeper lay half-sunk on a sandbar, but two of her guns still fired at the Stukas that broke through the RAF umbrella. A pier on the south end of the beach swarmed with men, but in the water, long queues snaked out from the shore, patiently waiting for the next rescuer.

A ship's boat motored from the stranded minesweeper to the incoming boats. A young man wearing a helmet, life jacket, sweater, and shorts, looking grimy and tired, hailed *Marbury Rose* while perched precariously on the boat's prow. Edmund heaved-to, hoping the boats behind would do the same. "*Ho* there," the young man shouted over the din of engines and popping ack-ack, "is this your first trip?"

"Aye," Edmund shouted back, "where do we start?"

"Start with the nearest queue. Pick up wounded first if you can. Are you armed?"

"Nay. Should we be?"

"If you're not armed, don't pick up any Germans: if you *are* armed, do as you like. Smaller vessels should ferry out to the larger ships off-shore, especially the wounded. Good luck to you." The grimy young man climbed down and motioned for his coxswain to return. *Marbury Rose* headed for the nearest queue a hundred yards off. As they drew near, they could make out men, sodden, hollow-eyed and dirty, chest-deep in cold, filthy water, holding their weapons out of the water and wounded over their heads. In her first stop, *Marbury Rose* took on fifty men and six litters—Welsh Borderers, Royal Artillerymen, and some engineers.

Grace helped a Medical Corpsman from Cornwall with the wounded and sick. Hurt or well, they all sat or stood or lay about quietly. They muttered "thank you, miss," and "God bless you, miss," when she gave them blankets, cigarettes, tea, cocoa, water, or anything else that was on-board to be offered. She cheerily asked those that seemed the most lucid if they knew where Colin's battalion was. The answer was always "no, miss" or "sorry, miss," and the speaker looked away to the shore, or a shake of the head and the same, pained glance away.

When *Marbury Rose* delivered her first load to a corvette already swarming with men, the able-bodied went up the scramble-nets as the others were helped. The litters were hoisted up by a hundred hands. Ship's boats and rafts hovered about already laden but taking on what they could. An ensign called down from the corvette's side. "Do you *need* anything?"

"Blankets," Grace called up, "and something hot to feed them, if you please." Several heads turned to look.

"You've got a *woman* down there," the ensign called back, querulously.

"Yes, *all* the boys say the same thing," Edmund answered. "Irish blood in the family, you know. Otherwise, she'd as soon not be here as *any* of us." This was met with general laughter. "About the blankets..."

"Yes, of course," the ensign replied, "and something hot as well. Half a tick." As the last of the men hauled aboard the corvette, a bundle of blankets swung out on a davit followed by a large urn of steaming liquid. "The cooks call it soup," the ensign called down. Thus provisioned, Grace and Edmund threw off the lines and headed for the beach again.

The first trip blended into the twentieth, long into the night and into the next day, and into the next. *Marbury Rose* tied up in the lee of a destroyer the second night, too weary to go on. On the third night, *Rose* was accompanied by a minelayer back to Ramsgate for fuel while ferrying a group of senior Belgian and French officers. When they started the next morning again, the queues seemed just as long, the noise from the beach just as loud. The *Luftwaffe* swept the beach with machine guns and dropped bombs.

The Cornish medic was still with them, tending to the wounded, replenishing the meager supplies, clearing off debris. It occurred to Grace that they didn't even know his name. Bandages, uniform parts, cigarette butts, blankets, and mugs were scattered about the previously pristine yacht.

And Uncle Edmund had taken such pride in the cleanliness of his Rose, Grace thought...

At one unclear time, a Lewis gun on a shoulder-high pedestal mount had been fastened to the roof of *Rose*'s cockpit, standing silent guard. An RAF armorer declared it operational, demonstrating its use. As they approached a queue that morning, three German fighters broke through the low-lying scud, spraying the sea with machine-gun fire. Grace leaped onto the roof, spun the machine gun around, braced against the recoil, and let fly with short bursts as if at geese over the heather. She turned the weapon as fast as she could, barely controlling the heavy gun's recoil.

Watching the long streamers of tracers arching up after the planes, she clamped down hard on the trigger, and it shook so violently she thought she'd chipped a tooth. An instant later, one plane's engine cowling ruptured, and black smoke belched from it. As the Messerschmitt passed over, she swung the gun to follow. There was another belch of smoke, a ball of flame, and the plane side-slipped down into the water, skipping twice before vanishing beneath the cold waves.

As one, the beach and water cheered, and ships sounded whistles and horns. "Hurrah!" Edmund yelled, "Three cheers and a tiger for us! Mark up a Hun for the House of Henley and *Marbury Rose*! Hurrah!"

"Good shooting, laddie," boomed a distinctly Highland voice from a nearby queue. "Ye potted 'im good, ye did! To the *Devil* with ye, infernal *blaggard*!"

"*Lassie*, if you *don't* mind," Grace yelled back, "but thank you, kind sir!" In gumboots and a filthy sweater, Grace executed the most elegant ballroom curtsy she had ever performed...on a rolling yacht roof.

The cheering that followed was distinctly heard miles inland.

• • •

It was that last trip back from that war-torn shore—six days and five nights after they started—that stayed in Grace's mind. *Marbury Rose* was fully laden with some of the only rear-guards that would get off the beach, the headquarters section of a Highland battalion, many of them wounded. By then, the fighting around the shrinking perimeter could clearly be heard, and although they hadn't been told officially, the flotilla knew this was the end.

Grace had stopped asking about Colin long before, who had been her original reason for going to that cold, terrifying shore. Somehow the idea of looking for her childhood friend and one-time beau got lost in long lines of struggling, wet, hurt, weary men, gunfire, air attacks, and the minor legend of *Annie Oakley of Dunkirk*. The French shore was a faint line on the horizon, and the men grew sullen and quiet. The glow of cupped cigarettes and the occasional heavy sigh were all that distinguished the sodden, exhausted soldiers from inanimate objects in the dark.

One boy had lost both legs at the hip and was strapped to a litter, full of morphine and raging with fever. Grace sat with him in the crowded cockpit, stroking his head, muttering soothing words. He suddenly reached up for her head. "I'm all right, miss," he said quite clearly, running his shaking, dirty fingers through her disheveled hair. "I'm all right. I'm all right. I'm all...oh...," and he died, clutching her hair with his last breath.

"Colin," someone called, "Colin, are you there?"

"Was *that* his name? Colin? Was that *his* name," Grace asked the voice; the name sounded familiar.

"Aye, it was miss," came the answer. "Colin McGuire of Shetland."

"Goodbye, then, Colin McGuire of Shetland," she whispered, folding his hands over his chest. "May you find rest." Only the rumbling of the engines and the lapping of the sea could be heard.

"Didn't he have a wife, then, Adam," another asked.

"Aye, he did," said another voice, "and two bairns as I recall. Pity." And the cockpit was silent once more. After a few minutes, Grace went out on the deck and stared out at the black, cold sea, crying silent tears, wondering if her Colin too had died, alone, among strangers.

• • •

It was near midnight when *Marbury Rose* hove to at the Ramsgate seawall. A harbor tug took her towline of four smaller boats. The men got off quietly, and each thanked Edmund and Grace with a nod or a tip of the headgear. Ambulances hauled off the litters, and a truck appropriately painted black took the dead boy away. Silently the rest fell into a formation of four ragged ranks. When the sergeant had taken the roll, he reported to his major, "*Forty-four* present, *sixteen* in hospital, *nineteen* dead, *eighty* missing, *SAH*!"

"*Very* good, Sergeant-Major. My lord, miss," he called out to Edmund and Grace, "if you would be so kind as to join us." Puzzled, Grace and her uncle clambered up to the formation. "We would be honored if you would accept induction."

"It's a *great* honor, Grace, the highest they can give. Just accept," Edmund whispered.

"Yes," they answered, "We accept."

"Grand. Sergeant-Major, inform the Clans. By the authority vested in me, I declare that from this day forward...ah, your *baptismal name*, my lord?"

"Edmund Alistair Fredrick Branson-Goshen."

"Yes: Edmund Alistair Fredrick Branson-Goshen, Duke of Mayfield and Peer of the English Realm, and Miss...?"

"Grace Margaret Henley of Cornwall."

"Yes: Grace Margaret Henley of Cornwall, are to be regarded as Kinsmen of the Clans of the Black Watch and are to be granted all honors and privileges of other kinsmen. So, then, Sergeant Major, is there a wee dram among us?"

The old NCO spun on his heel. "Campbell! Your flask!" In smart military fashion, a burly corporal with a hurt arm and a machine gun on his shoulder marched up and thrust a silver bottle forward. "Cognac will have to do, *SAH*!"

The flask was passed around, each swigging of the thick liqueur, reciting their clan names. "Campbell... MacLeish... Frasier... McDermott...," one by one, each name symbolizing the acceptance of their ancient clans.

"Sergeant-Major," the major called out again, the flask put away, "up the street to the left we've billets for the night. *March* the men to quarters. *O'Bannon*, you renegade Irishman, *they* don't know we're *here* yet: *Scots Wa Hae!* Pipe our dead through Hell and let Saint Peter know they're coming on to Him." Then, turning to Edmund and Grace, "Thank you for our lives, my lord, miss. You're one with our clans now. Goodbye and keep well. Now *sing*, lads; *SING!*"

Scots, who have with Wallace bled,
Scots, whom Bruce has often led,
Welcome to your gory bed
Or to victory.

He marched after his men, their lusty song echoing in the dark night, bagpipe skirling in the blackness, the heavy tread of their marching feet resonating in the shadows.

Old Salt

With apologies to the men of the Operation PEDESTAL convoy and SS Ohio...

The Three Anchors Saloon, for some unfathomable reason, is famous for shanty stories, though it's no different, better, or worse than any other saloon on the edge of any other harbor anywhere in the world. With no pool table, TV, darts, pinball, or any of the other trappings of other dram shops, it seems natural that the patrons entertain themselves with yarns.

We heard *this* story on one of those magical, payday-weekend, new-ships-in-harbor spring nights when even the wharves that always smelled of bilge and fuel oil had the scent of new life in the air. At the Three Anchors, a bunch of us regulars—dock rats and hangers-on mostly, and no more than one in ten of us was a regular sailor of any sort—were listening intently to the newcomers who were buying drinks and spinning yarns of daring-do on the high seas.

One of the newcomers on this particular night, a first-rate seaman named Ned, told a tale about the Falklands when he was a hand on *Atlantic Conveyor*. He talked about that tub like it was the most important in the world, which, of course, for him, it *was*.

One of the regulars, an old, old seaman we knew only as Thomas, sipped his free beer from the shadows of the end of the bar, staring into space, listening. When Ned had finished up—with *Atlantic Conveyor* catching an Exocet meant for a carrier and going down—Thomas cleared off his stool in the shadows and hove-to alongside the jukebox. He beckoned in that international gesture of yarn-spinners the world and ages over to come hither for a tale of heroes and heroism. That none of us had ever before heard him speak of any vessel he'd served on gave him a feel of intrigue.

And after he started, his demeanor changed from that of a storyteller to a survivor reliving an event...having an audience didn't matter. We *knew* we were about to hear one of those stories you hear just once but never repeat, reserving its private resurrection from the dark recesses of your mind on those special occasions when all seems lost, and then only as a reminder of what a *rough go* is really about.

His tale went like this...

I lost a ship once, on the Gibraltar to Malta run back in '42. I was skipper of *Standard New Jersey*, the biggest tanker in the world at the time...

First day out, our convoy had eighteen ships, all heavy-laden except the one slated to be the rescue ship. None of us had sailed that route yet during the war, but the escort and the convoy commander had told us to expect trouble. And brother, were *they* right.

Standard New Jersey was laden with bunker oil and aviation gas. Under normal conditions, nobody in their right minds would put the two on the same ship. But Malta needed that juice, so the Brits leased her to carry the stuff in. The owners told me to keep my vessel safe for as long as I could, and for the twenty-odd years I'd been with the company, I always tried to do what they asked me to...

Anyway, we sailed with the tide off of Gibraltar on a cloudy morning in late June, headed east into the sun, trying to avoid the African coast as much as possible. The escorts started to thin out the first night since nobody wanted to risk the aircraft carriers in those waters. Risk the carriers?! Ha! What the hell were they doing with eighteen merchant vessels if not risking them? Well, I ask ya...

About an hour into the third watch, it started, and lit up a general stores ship to the north. Don't know the name; never asked. Been on enough convoys to know that it didn't really matter. We just adjusted course away from the wreck and pushed on at ten knots...

Now, *Standard New Jersey* could do *twenty* knots without straining a rivet. Still, there were old coal-fired ships with us that were huffing at ten. You *know* a convoy dare not outrun its slowest members. So, there we were in Nazi-infested waters dawdling along about as fast as a schoolchild can run for ice cream, with a few million pounds of fuel oil and avgas, just waiting for some Kraut with a torpedo to blow us to kingdom come...

Probably another hour after that, there's this bloody great explosion off our starboard beam, and this 20,000 tonner goes down without a trace: no wreckage, no fire, no survivors. Ammunition ship, you see. Probably took a torpedo in the central hold. They'll do that...

Not too much else happened that first night. We heard the escorts over the radio running off after contacts, but nothing else went up. Settled in on the zigzag pattern and tried to get some shuteye. Figured I'd need it come morning...

Got up just as the east started to get light. Ordered all hands to mess and stations because I knew we were out of the range of fighter protection from Gibraltar, and we were days from the cover of Malta. I ordered the boats swung out, and the rafts unlashed, set on the deck. The funny thing is I'd never ordered anything of the sort before on *Standard New Jersey*. Not much sense, really. Ya see you can't hardly get away from a torpedoed tanker, 'cause they just light up like the Fourth of July. You put the boats out in *that* River Styx of burning cargo, and…*you* get it. And Carley floats, well, they're only balsa wood...

Not a half-hour after sunrise, we saw the first big four-engine spotter planes. Some of the merchant ships started shooting, but the escorts and the smart skippers got them to stop. They were way out of range, ya see, and only wanting to send the count and the location back to their buddies. It wasn't them Condors that we worried about; it was them *little* bastards with the screaming wings and the big bombs that blow a ship's bottom out that you wanted to shoot at...

Standard Ohio was in the middle of the formation, a privileged position because of her cargo and sheer size. If anyone wanted to get any more convoys into Malta, Malta had to have avgas, and *Standard Ohio* was carrying more avgas than the other tankers in that convoy put together.

Ya know, sometimes I gotta wonder if the other ships in that convoy weren't just out there as bait to draw the wolves to *them*, so's just a few ships got through. One of 'em was supposed to be *Standard New Jersey*...

It didn't take long for the wolves to start to circle. Trimotors at first, Eyeties. Got better range than the Stukas and carry a bigger wallop in them torpedoes. At first, they just did a circuit around us, out of range, sizing up their quarry. Always felt kinda helpless when they did that, just wished they'd come in and be done with it...

But see, they were smart, yessir, *real* smart. When they pointed their noses in at us, our two CAM ships fired off their fighters to try and bag those big Eyeties before they got too close in. Eyeties knew that, or at least the Kraut giving the orders knew that, so the big Trimotors just peeled off to home, and them clapped-out ol' Hurricanes had nowhere to go but the drink and nothin' to shoot at. They stayed up as long as they could, spotting for the convoy. In time, they had to come down. We picked up one of the pilots, but we had no more fighters, and the Krauts knew it...

Then the fun began. First off the bat, we saw a swarm of Stukas head in for us. But our gunners—we had twin 20-millimeter guns, fore and aft, and a 3-inch on the center deck—held fire until they were committed to their target, then let 'em *have* it. Boy, what shooting they did! Yessir, right nice it was. Got two of them Huns before we got the first near miss, just off the port bow. Didn't do anything but scratch the paint, but it sure was scary seeing that big egg falling in your direction...

Other guys weren't so lucky. A tanker astern of us got one amidships, went up like a Roman candle. Kerosene, ya see. Another one ahead got one in the bow, nearly took that bow off. Still fighting her when we passed. Our big eight-inch escorting cruiser got a near-miss that she just shook off, and another little corvette got blown in half. Sea started filling with junk and oil and floats and bodies. Never saw the like before. Never *want* to again...

When ships went down in the Atlantic, the convoys were further apart, and you never saw the remains. But in the Malta convoys, the ships were closer together for flak protection. Depended on each other's guns, ya see. And besides, the sea's a *lot* rougher in the big water—Mediterranean's like a millpond in summer in comparison—smooth, flat, quiet. You got to see all that was left of ships when they bought it...

That air attack sank three ships, so we closed in on the remainder. The Krauts come back a few minutes later with more bombs, and this time the Eyeties come back with 'em. They bore in hell-bent for election, and we shoot back. A half-hour later, we're down two more hulls, and three more escorts have bought it. We close in like sheep, hoping our shepherds will come and rescue us. We pick up a half-dozen boats and pluck a few poor buggers outta the drink, all covered with oil and spitting up seawater and guts...

It's the oil, ya see. The fuel oil gets to your insides and eats at 'em like acid. Your ship gets hit; it leaks its own fuel. Ten feet thick, in some places. Hard to swim in, too. Bound to end up swallowing some, or worse, inhaling some. Seven sailors died in my wardroom that day, eaten up by fuel oil, or bled to death. Had one poor bastard that caught fire before he went into the drink. He was still smoldering when we picked him up. He gurgled for another hour out on the deck with no skin left, lungs full of fluid, guts fried, blind. Didn't stand a snowball's chance in Hell of living another day, so the Doc just loaded up his hypo and gave us, and him, some peace. Oh, yeah, I know what you're thinking. "You killed one of ours," you say. Sure, and I'd do 'er again, too, says I. In a minute, I would.

Anyway, the surviving escorts are running around like hens with a weasel in the coop, wearing out their crews. I was on the bridge with the convoy commander, both of us praying for night, so all we have to worry about was U-boats picking off cripples. By noon we've had at least half the convoy hit, and brother, there's no end in sight. More trimotors hit us before dark, and the Stukas again. Most of the real old tubs on the outside of the convoy had been sunk or crippled by then, so most of what was left was newer, bigger ships that at least could take some damage and move faster. We increased the convoy's speed to fifteen knots as we passed by another tanker just as the watch changed. She'd caught three torpedoes and two bombs. Burning like a bonfire, she was...

A tanker's compartmented like a maze to keep the liquid from sloshing around in heavy seas. Well, what *that* means is that unless her bottom's blown entirely out, or she's opened up from stem to stern, a tanker can take a week to sink. If she catches fire, she'll be burning all the while...

By sundown we were still a day out of air cover. I looked at the barometer and saw that we were headed into a storm; we'd be in it maybe sometime the next day. The convoy commander thinks this is a chance for us to make a dash straight into Malta. *Standard New Jersey* could have made it on her own in a straight line in a little over seventeen hours from where we were, maybe less. But breaking up the convoy was a mighty desperate thing to do, especially when there's a threat of air attack. So we think about it for a while and try not to want to do it too much...

Two hours into the evening watch, it happened, and I *still* can't remember where I was at the time. Long after the war, somebody figured we'd hit a mine that the Eyeties had dropped in front of the convoy. Anyway, there was this goddamn big explosion on the starboard side aft, and the first thing I can remember is sliding down the stairwell to the forward fire room. There were steam and smoke everywhere, some fuel coming in from the forward bulkhead, and some seawater from a few seams. I go back aft, and the chief engineer tells me the after fireroom is full of water, and the main engine room is about hip deep. I ran my hand up against a bulkhead, and it was cold as a witch's tit in a brass bra when it should have been hotter than hell. Engine room called in and said they were still getting steam. Deck watch said we'd started to lose cargo...

My first instinct was to try to pump the after fireroom clean but decided we'd need all the power from the shafts we could get. I set the auxiliary pumps to do the job and went back topside—nothing we could do about a hole in our side except keep going. A solo dash for Malta was out, though...

Now, a tanker can shift one liquid cargo for another and mix the two...if needed. I took it into my head to combine the avgas and the bunker oil, cutting down on the chances of an explosion if we got hit again. It can be done, but it takes time. Didn't want to do it before if I didn't have to because it's a lot of trouble to separate the two. I told myself they'd rather have *mixed* juice than *no* juice at all, so I told the cargo officer to get it done. Three hours later, we got this nasty, semi-volatile fuel in all the holds, but at least we won't blow up if somebody sneezed too hard.

At fifteen knots (we were straining a bit by then, but not too bad), we were too fast for subs but not for motor torpedo boats. We saw one flotilla that the escorts chased away, so we managed to avoid more trouble. At dawn, the sun came up through a dark cloud bank. The storm we saw coming the night before was gonna hit us soon, and hopefully, the buzzards weren't gonna be able to take off. But, no such luck. They were at us before we could change the morning watch, and brother was they mad. Came at us like hornets...

I remember a bomb hit just on the fo'c'sle, and I was on the bridge aft. The bow gun and the gunners just vanished. Just a few minutes later, there was another near miss just off our stern. Rudder control was gone, and we were on fire in the forward mess. The main engine room had more water coming in. We were losing power fast...

Then this Eyetie trimotor flies over our deck real low, and I remember thinking that we were dead. It was just that simple. Then I hear this great THUD amidships on our port side, and the cargo officer says we're losing cargo again. I go over to look, and there's a great gash just below the waterline, pumping out oil like a hose. I say shut off the port side tanks and pump in seawater. I wanted to flush the tank, so I could put a patch on the hole...

Then there was this explosion, and I looked around and saw that the entire aft superstructure was on fire. Didn't know it just then, but I found out later that when the fire hit the galley, the cooking gas flashed back and blew up the tanks. Now we had a fire from port to starboard in the *only* shelter we were gonna have, and we were headed into a storm...

We put all hands to the fires, three of 'em now, left a skeleton crew below decks to run the engines and work on the other damage. We trunked the auxiliary pumps to one of the firefighting lines and brought out oil-laden water from the after fire room. That sludge was *not* good to *fight* fires with, but it cooled the structure to keep the fire from spreading—bunker oil won't flash. By this time, we'd fallen out of the convoy because we could barely make steerageway. We weren't sinking, oh, no; we were *burning* and losing power. I had half a mind to put most of the crew off and try to get her in with a skeleton, not that there was much chance of that then. The convoy commander had a destroyer come alongside so he could take his flag off. It was sad, really. He'd wanted to stay, but he had the other ships to think of. Everybody thought our tub was a goner. We put our badly wounded on the destroyer when he went. We shook hands, said, "see you in Valletta," but I'm not sure either one of us expected to, really. I sure as hell didn't...

About then, we reached the storm, and we had water coming in everywhere because the overheads were all burned off or caved in. We raised steerageway and got on course again. We finally got the after fireroom pumped out enough to get in, but it was a mess. The mine had gone off three feet below the waterline to starboard, and with a hole on the *other* side, we couldn't list her enough to close it. The second hole was big enough to drive a Duesenberg through, clean in the middle of the bunker. A busted seam was what flooded the fire room. All I could think to do was to put some guys on it, just to keep them busy. Had enough to think about without the convoy around and still half a day away from fighter cover...

We pumped water, fought fires, patched seams, got wet. We still had twenty sound seamen left, and I'd only lost one officer. The sky was this leaden grey color that means rain for an hour...or a week...and the sea was starting to foam. The wind wasn't that bad, but any rain is *mighty* cold when you haven't eaten or slept in a day or more...

We were making pretty good time when the Stukas paid us another visit. This time I figured we were goners, sure, and so did everybody else. I ordered an erratic zigzag with the engines, but we were sluggish with two holes in us. We'd managed to overpressure the central port hold enough to get a tar patch over the hole, but it would leak anyway, and we couldn't maintain air pressure to keep the water out. The Stukas came at us bow-to-stern, one at a time. Our three-inch popped off, and the stern 'twenties did what they could, but it just wasn't enough. The first bomb splashed off the port side, the second hit in the fo'c'sle but didn't go off, the third dropped through the weather deck and went off right at the junction of all four central holds amidships. Took out the cargo pumps and the 3-incher too. Right then, I knew we were a dead ship...

We started to leak cargo out of both sides, with seams popped out ten feet high. We blew out the tar patch and began to list to port, and couldn't stop it. We were still making way, so I thought, "To Hell with 'em all. I'm gonna bring this tub in if it kills me." We were a day away from Valletta at our speed then, and I figured I'd just go as far and as fast as I could...

We lost the radio when the superstructure lit up, so we couldn't talk to anyone. We didn't know right then that the rest of the convoy, a little better than a third of the ships, was even then getting in. The Admiralty had written us off as a loss, and Malta was trying to figure out how to go on without avgas. I heard later that Churchill was quietly discussing abandoning the Rock just because *Standard New Jersey* didn't make it in...

But ya see *Standard New Jersey* was never any ordinary vessel. *Standard New Jersey* was the largest vessel afloat in terms of displacement, a kind of model for the real big brutes you see nowadays that are so big they never see port between launching and scrapping, and she was carrying a hundred and twenty million pounds of bunker fuel and avgas. If it took a week to sink any ordinary tanker, it would take a month to sink *her*, unless she blew up. *I* knew that, the *crew* knew that, the *builders* and the *owners* knew it, but damn few *others* did...

So I cracked the throttles wide, dodged in and out of squalls, and pumped out water to correct the list. We fought fires of burning metal that just wouldn't go out, topped off the cargo with seawater, patched the hull, fixed the pumps, and every now and again dodged the occasional bomb. Worked like dogs we did, every last one of us. I hadn't done so much with my hands since I stood engineering watches, I swear. The storm line stayed with us long enough to hide us from the Krauts most of the time, but we could hear 'em swarming around out there. Every now and again, they'd drop in through a hole in the clouds. Since they were near-vertical on their descent and we were so low in the water, their aim was way off. A couple of 'em didn't pull out, just flew right down into the drink...

The next morning the bow watch saw land, and a few minutes later, this flying boat came over us for a look-see. I imagine we were quite a sight, water sixteen feet from the thwarts when it should've been thirty-five, all the structure burned off, trailing fuel like a stuck pig trails blood, but we were making headway. The next thing I knew, we were surrounded by Hurricanes and Spitfires and motorboats, everybody waving and hollering and jumping up and down. We just looked at them kinda dumb like, wondering what all the excitement was about.

Ya see, we were the last tanker left outta that convoy, and we were carrying the hope of the whole of Malta in our holds. We had serious freeboard problems by then, and I knew we couldn't negotiate the tricky entrance to the Grand Harbor without rudder control, and there weren't enough big tugs to push us. I did the only thing I knew to do—I beached her.

Once ashore, that convoy commander pumped my hand up and down like a long-lost brother, did a little jig. I cabled the owners and waited for instructions since the contract was done. The owners were relieved that I was alive and that *Standard New Jersey* was at least salvageable. I didn't have the heart to tell them that she would probably spend the rest of her life as a beached whale. Couldn't, anyway. Classified, ya know...

Yup, I lost my last ship. I spent the rest of the war organizing and commanding convoys after the Coast Guard gave me a Commodore's commission. The Brits hung a medal on me, and the Maltese gave me an honorary knighthood. We brought in about three months' worth of avgas, and that was *another* three months that the Krauts had to run OUR gauntlet, the one Malta put up between North Africa and Sicily. It was *the* three months before Monty hit Rommel where it hurt at El Alamein.

I haven't had a ship of my own since. I read a few years back where they finally hauled the hulk of *Standard New Jersey* off that damn beach and scrapped her. I read too that the day she beached is still considered a national holiday for Malta. I'm invited back for some celebration every year, and every year I turn them down. The only time I want to go back there is when they spread my ashes in the Med, right there where I brought her in.

Remembering all those good men who died bringing her in ain't all that tough for me. Commemorating it with brass bands and speeches and waving flags, now that just doesn't make much sense. Being here on a night like this, with guys like you, now *that's* a commemoration in my book. *You* understand. *You'll* never forget.

All them others, they *need* reminders every year.

Lifesaver

**_I got a version of this story from the mother of a friend of mine who was a
Red Cross Volunteer_**

There were fifty gals—women, but *most* were girls—on a liner in late '42.
The fast liners didn't need convoys, but ours—SS *Golden Star*–wasn't *quite*
that fast. We were nurses mostly, a few of the early WACs and WAVEs, Red
Cross girls like me, some USO girls, and a few others. Imagine fifty girls on
an ocean voyage for two weeks with a thousand boys. They didn't put up
with any hanky-panky in those days, so, other than a *little* flirting in the
mess, there was practically no contact between us. *Golden Star* was on the
tail end of the convoy and one of the designated rescue ships since they
figured we could stop and catch up again if we had to. I never thought it
could get so noisy at sea. Engines racing and slowing, zig-zagging into the
sea, and back running with it again. This was a big convoy, so there were a
lot of ships in it.

Three nights out of port, just after dark, there was this big KABOOM! We
go out on deck, and the ship just ahead of us had got a torpedo. Escorts were
already dropping depth charges off to the north, and a couple others were
coming alongside the cripple. But the escorts had to stand off again 'cause
that ship took *another* torpedo. But she was just a freighter, with only thirty
or so guys aboard, so we all got underway soon after, knowing she was a
goner.

Just thirty guys...they were *only* thirty out of thirty *thousand* people in the
convoy. Then one of the escorts got blown in half about a thousand yards in
front of me...and *vanished*. Then, somewhere ahead of us, there was *another*
explosion...and *another*...and *another*...

We turned in, but we couldn't sleep much. After a few hours, I gave up
and went back up on deck with a couple other adventurous gals. One—Helen
Borchardt, one of the first Army nurses commissioned—had a habit of
reaming out men who didn't salute her. She always said it was because there
would be other women after her that may not have the sand to tell men that
women could be officers, too.

We're up on the quarterdeck when we head for a ship that got a torpedo in
her forward hold and was sinking slowly. She'd taken on survivors of the

two *other* ships, and now *they* had to go into the drink again. *Golden Star* slowed to a stop. We rolled the scramble-net down into the water, and that ship—she was a troopship, *Rockbridge County*—was already putting boats off. We were lowering boats when *Rockbridge County's* whistle started to blow, and all of a sudden, everybody got into an all-fired hurry. We asked what the panic was, and a sailor told us that they lock the whistle down when the water reaches the fire rooms to relieve steam pressure fast *without* cooking the crew.

Then, Helen says, "*Come on*, girls, *work* to be done," and she leads us down to the deck where the guys are coming aboard. We start with the usual blankets and water, then the ship's doctor comes up and starts in with his pharmacist's mates. Most of their patients are the guys that came over in boats. Most of them are dirty, tired, and cold, and a few have injuries...

Now I'd seen men get caught in cotton gins and grain elevators, and I'd spent a couple years in nurse's college by then. But in a few minutes, we started pulling boys out of the water, with injuries the likes of which I'd *never* seen...

It was the smell that got to me, I think. The smell of bunker oil and vomit, blood and seawater, burned hair, and burned paint that those boys carried with them was just overwhelming. It was too dark out to see much, but we could *smell* them, *hear* them...the small voices of boys crying, with that *godawful* whistle *screeching* in the background, and the steam ripping the ship apart. I thought I'd retch, so I went over to the rail, and I looked out across the water. *Rockbridge County* was going down at the bow, and the water was full of those little salt-water lights bobbing in the swells, winking like stars. Each one of those lights was another boy in the drink.

I don't think I've ever seen anything quite so lonely as a ship sinking at night. The ocean is like liquid cold black eternity made blacker by the reflection of the burning ship, those salt-water lights, and the burning oil on the surface. It's almost as if the world took all the light and warmth away 'cause a dying ship didn't need it anymore. I couldn't help but think that I should do *something* for the boys in the water. I knew I'd be no good on deck, but I was a pretty strong swimmer, so I threw off my greatcoat and life preserver and grabbed one of the hand lines over the side and tied it around me and between my legs, then climbed down the side of the net and into the drink.

In a few seconds, I went numb from the chest down, but I started to haul boys towards the net who were worn out from the swim in the cold water. Boats were herding them in like sheep. All I could see were the bobbing lights and grey lumps moving towards me. I'd pull one boy into the net, then another, and another. Finally, I'm just hanging on the net, getting them started up, with this rope between my legs that I couldn't feel anymore. My hands were just frozen hooks. Sometimes I'd haul in a boy so severely burned his skin would just come off in my hands when I let go, but I kept on dragging 'em in.

While I was doing *that, Rockbridge County* sank...

When I climbed up, the boats were being hauled in, and most of the boys were already on deck. When I couldn't see any more lights, I managed to climb up to the deck—a neat trick when you can't feel your feet. Two boys grabbed me by the arms and dragged me over the rail. Some medical corpsman came over with a flashlight and started to look me over.

I was numb from the neck down, covered with fuel oil, and my nightshirt was gathered up around my armpits. Mind you that when I'd got up out of bed, I just pulled a pair of pants on under my nightshirt, so no *bra*, no *panties*, no *nothing*.

As soon as they untied the rope around me, my pants fell down around my ankles. So here's half the Navy staring at my oil-covered *boobs* and half the Army staring at my oil-covered *crotch,* and this poor guy suddenly realized what he'd done and pretended I wasn't there but *still* held the flashlight on me! Fortunately, it was a *red-filtered* light, so I was just a dark blob…*curvy*, maybe, but a blob without details.

In a matter of seconds—that felt like hours—Helen came over, wrapped a blanket around me, and hustled me into a shower. The doctor came by a little later and checked me out. But for the rest of the crossing, I got some *very* peculiar looks from some of the guys.

The corpsman with the flashlight was Max Fenwell from Boston. We wrote. He couldn't apologize enough for what he'd done, and I kept telling him to forget it. He eventually went to the Pacific. I got a letter from his mother after he got killed off Okinawa. She said he'd intended to marry me when the war was over, and she wanted me to know.

I finished my nursing degree after the war. I went to Korea after I joined the Army Nurse Corps in '50, then I did a tour in Germany from '55 to '58, then I was in Vietnam '67-'68, and again '70 to '71. I retired from the Nurse Corps in '80.

I've thought about that dark water and the cold, and Max from time to time. *Guys*, sure, lots of 'em. Married? I was *close* a couple times, but then I'd see the life leaving *Rockbridge County*, as the dark ocean swallowed her up, and those lights struggling to safety.

Someone had to go out and save them.

I decided that *someone* was to be *me*.

To Rest with Long Ears

**If you believe in forever, then governments and bureaucracy are eternal.
But sometimes they screw up and get something done**

Part of a speech given by Eli Soden in June 196-
"...And as I reach the autumn of my life, despite all the honors given me
by my friends, comrades, and, yes, my enemies, it is my fondest wish to rest,
finally, with Long Ears."

Memo from the Governor in July 196-
...For all that he's done for the state, I'd think it appropriate. Trouble is,
what the *Hell* does he *mean* by "to rest with Long Ears?"

*Transcript from a taped interview of George Thunderman in September
196-*
"Nope, sorry. Long Ears don't ring no bells. *Might* have something to do
with Korea. I know he went there, was there for near a year back in '50-51.
But that was before I knew him. Find somebody who knew him in Korea;
maybe they can help."

*Fragment of the report, Center for Native American Studies in September
196-*
Considering the status of subject Soden in his clan as a shaman of the
Apache religion, the likeliest meaning of the cryptic fragment "to rest" is
probably buried. "Long Ears," however, has no special meaning that we can
decipher.

*Raw tape interview fragment of an interview with Alicia Soden in October
196-*
Q: Any ideas as to what your father means by "Long Ears"?

A: A couple. Once, Tommy, my brother, wanted to name some mangy cur
with big floppy ears that. He was twelve, and I was fifteen, I think, so this
would be about '60 or so. Anyway, Dad got all upset, said it was an insult to
our ancestors or something like that. Started chanting and dancing like I
hadn't seen him do in ages. I figured it was something religious, but I never
knew that much about Dad's faith.

Q: Anything else?

A: Well, *Mom's* reaction was odd, I think. Usually, she just said "Cool it,"
or whatever it was she said then, but not *this* time. *This* time she got all hot

and bothered, said we couldn't name *any* dog that. Got scared, and *that* was bizarre. We named the dog Bottles, though I can't remember *why*...

Q: You have another idea?

A: About Long Ears? Well, my folks went on a cruise across the Pacific for their 25th anniversary back in '65. The state and a whole lot of people pitched in just after Dad was named Chief of Tribal Police. They stopped off at Easter Island, and Mom said Dad just stared at the statues for half a day. You know the ones in the pictures? With the real weird ears...?

Fragment of a letter from Cadet Thomas Soden dated October 196-

In re your query of August 196-,...Mother would have been the best source, but she passed just after they returned from the Pacific, as you know... I suggest you contact Emil Ridgely, his oldest friend, or Sam Waterman, a comrade in the National Guard, on the Long Ears question.

From an interview with Emil Ridgely MD, December 196-

I'm not sure, really. I do remember once talking about Korea a few years after he got back...he was real cagey about it...had to pull every word out of him...

From the statement of Sam Waterman, December 196-

Long Ears is not a familiar name to me, but I didn't meet Eli until 1954. It may have been after that...I suggest you contact Deke Wallace. I think they were together in the Detachment before the war...the Korean war, that is...

Taped interview fragment, National Guard Bureau records search from January 196-

Yes, *here* we are...Elijah Soder, *Lakota* was his Apache birth name— Quiet One. At seventeen, he became *Varlebena Lichánee Ndeeń* or Forever Dog Man. He enlisted in March 1941, drafted to Federal service in May 1942, and served in...*this* is odd: he served in North Africa and Italy. Most code-talkers went to the Pacific with...oh, *that's* why. He was with Detachment I, 200th Military Police Battalion....of *course*. Arizona and New Mexico National Guardsmen formed the nucleus... No, nothing on *anyone* named Long Ears here…but *our* records only cover until they were drafted, really...It doesn't cover replacements...

From the newspaper archives of the Nashville (TN)Tribune, 16 March 196-

I've found something that may be of interest to you: a newspaper story about an Indian named Soder and his tracker dog named Long Ears...

Clipping from Nashville Tribune, *dated 12 August 1940*

The notorious killer George "Strangler" Bannerman, wanted throughout the South for a series of vicious, savage crimes, has been brought to the bar of justice with the aid of an Apache boy and his faithful bloodhound...After six weeks of tracking Bannerman and his band of cutthroats across fever swamps, through torrential rains, and over treacherous mountains, only seventeen-year-old Soder and his dog Long Ears could follow the trail...Bannerman was the only member of his gang to survive the climactic gun duel that ended his terrible reign as the scourge of the law-abiding...

Memo from Atlanta Federal Prison archives, dated September 1942

In his final hours, Bannerman admitted, and I quote: "I wake up in the middle of the night, and I see *them* there, in the shadows. I'll be glad to swing, just so's I won't see *them* every night..."

Interview with the Military History Division, US Army, dated 22 June 196-

Yes, 200th MP Battalion. *Great* outfit, as I recall. Formed of policemen from all over the country. Real professional cops, in demand in every theater. Detachments and even whole companies sent hither and yon. Let's see...Detachment I ...yes, *here* we are. Detachment I, formed in June 1942 at Hill Field, Utah. They were predominantly made up of tribal and reservation police in the Arizona and New Mexico Guard and organized into two sections: canine and sharpshooter. There are stories about them in Italy hitting targets a valley away, better than a *thousand* yards. And the trackers: why, no one who they tracked *ever* got away, or so they *said...*

Fragment of the interview with Edward McCaffery (Public Safety Commissioner, City of Cincinnati) conducted 15 August 196-

Q: What do you remember of Detachment I?

A: The first time I saw them, I remember thinking: Oh, Jesus, Mary, and *Joseph*, McCaffery! *Get* your Mick ass down to the Provost Marshall and tell him you're *sorry*. Whatever it was that you did, you didn't deserve *this…*

I was just promoted to first lieutenant and was the only professional *military* policeman in the unit, and I was to teach these guys to be military cops. But I didn't really have anything to worry about. Somebody got smart and realized that they had real specialists here who could use existing talents like the code-talkers did. We turned them into *soldiers*, but they were still dog-handlers and sharpshooters in the end.

Q: What do you recall of Eli Soder in the tracker section?

A: I remember giving him a medal when he caught up to the Cairo Ripper. He tracked him across the Qatar Depression in Egypt, two hundred miles of sugar sand and salt, flat as a billiard table and a hundred fifty degrees at the surface. *Should* have killed them all, but he brought the Ripper back. And we hung *that* degenerate bastard.

Q: What about Long Ears?

A: That was the dog, of course. First canine I ever promoted, but not the last. Nossir, *not* the last.

Q: Promoted him to what?

A: Well, he was a buck sergeant at the time, and we raised him to staff sergeant.

Excerpt of a letter from Captain Leonard Massey, USA, Military Police, dated 5 September, 197-

Dogs are conferred rank and service numbers for several reasons. The most obvious is for accountability: we *have* to know how many to *feed*, and accounting *must* be made. The second is age. Most dogs' *effective* career in the Army is about five years, and any sentinel dog that's been promoted to platoon sergeant (that's three stripes and two rockers) has *probably* reached retirement age, and the Corps can track their age this way. In the case of *tracker* dogs, it's their relative merit. We use the canine promotion system to set values on a dog's skills...

Letter from Amadeus (Deke) Wallace, dated 19 August 197-

Yes, I served with Eli in Italy, North Africa, and Korea. Knew him quite well. Knew Long Ears, too. I was evacuated just before the roof caved in on us up on the Chongchon River in '50, so I don't *know* what happened to Long Ears, and Eli never told me. Eli and forty-six of us with three dogs were activated in July of '50, shipped off to Japan in August, shipped to Korea in October, and pulled out in December. Forty-four were still on their feet, and one *other* guy and I got evacuated. But the dogs were gone...

Fragment of the interview with Steven Thoms, Archivist in the National Archives, conducted 5 June 197-

Q: What have you got on Detachment I, 200th MP Battalion in Korea?

A: Not a damn thing: it looks like they disappeared about September of 1950. Just went *kapoof.*

Q: So when'd they get deactivated?

A: Stood down from federal orders March 1951 at Fort Hood, Texas. But between September and March, I've got nothing. I don't even know how they got from Japan to Texas, let alone if they *officially* got to Korea anyway. *Unofficially,* everybody was so concerned about getting warm bodies into Korea they'd take any outfit that was only half organized...

Letter from James Ingersoll, Professor of Military History, the University of Colorado, dated 19 September 197-

In response to your request for information on Detachment I, I'm afraid I'm as mystified as you are. While researching my part of the Army's Official History on the Military Police branch in World War II, I did run across Detachment I. I tried to follow them to Korea because they fascinated me. But I lost them when the archives did.

I did find something, though, that I have not yet followed up on. It seems that a Navy destroyer picked up some members of the Detachment off the eastern coast of Korea in late November and early December of 1950. Seems they got tied up with a little-heard-of outfit called the 90th Infantry Regiment. I've looked, and it's *not* in the Army's official roster, so it doesn't seem to be a heraldic unit. I hope this helps.

Entries in Ship's Log, USS Rowan *(DD214), 30 November 1950-1 December 1950*

1615 Hours 30 Nov: Took aboard parts of HHC 90th Infantry Regt. (USA), Lieut. Col. W. Toombs, Commanding, from N. Korean soil...Also [elements of] B Batty 555th AAA Bn., C/1st Bn 90th Inf, 321st Signals Det, S. African Air Force Ground Liaison, ROK 123rd Regt., Det I 200th MP Bn...66 persons...

2330 Hours: Provided gunfire support to 90th Regt. [Task Force Toombs]...

0800 Hours 1 Dec: Took aboard remainder of 90th Regt and attached units, 654th Eng. Bn.; 910th Maint. Bn.; 345th Tank Bn.; Det. I, 200th MP Bn;...41 persons.

1200 Hours: Burial at sea for 21 personnel, including Col. Ginty, Robt. L. Commander 90th Inf Regt. [killed in action on or about] 23 Nov; body contaminated and buried for sanitary reasons.

Letter from Alumni Locator, USMA West Point, dated 31 October 197-

We have *two* Toombs, W. for that period. One was branched to the Quartermasters and is now dead. The other was branched infantry and retired in Killen, Texas... I hope this helps...

Interview with Wiley Toombs, Lieutenant General USA (Ret) 28 November 197-

Q: Tell me about the 90th Infantry...

A: Why?

Q: Well, I'd like to know about an outfit it was tied up with...

Q: Why?

A: There was an NCO with the outfit, Eli Soder...

Q: Oh, *him*. Then you want to know about *Detachment I*...

A: Yessir.

Q: I'm sorry, son. I get that way when someone wants to talk about the old 90th. I got *so* tired of trying to defend that outfit. Ginty's family screeching about how he was murdered, and we hid the body. There's no records of the regiment left—*God*, what a mess that was. I've been cleaning it up since '51.

A: That's all right, sir. I'd just like to know about Soder and his dog...

Q: That bloodhound? Don't know quite what to say. Detachment I was assigned to HHC of the 90th when it formed in Japan. We were the only infantry regiment in the Army that had dogs assigned. Anyway, we shipped off to Korea about a month after Inchon, drove north as a kind of rear-area security behind X Corps. 90th *Regiment*? Christ, we only ever had two battalions and a headquarters, and all because the Ginty's HAD to have little Robert command his own regiment.

A: Yessir. About Soder...

Q: I'm getting there, son. We were up on the Chongchon when the Chinese came at us, and we woke up one morning, and we had contact with no one. We were stuck on a branch road that neither the Chinese nor the Korcoms wanted any part of. Anyway, we started south and picked up a South African FAC team who had communications with damn near anyone. By nightfall, we discovered we were the rearguard of the corps. Second Infantry division was getting cut to hell. We took on other lost outfits and pushed south. There was no question in my mind about surrendering. I'd spent three years in a German camp, and there was no way in *Hell* I was going to spend another minute behind barb wire. No Chinese to speak of came that close while we withdrew those first two nights.

After that, the Detachment would go out hunting at night. They had infrared scopes, see. And we had a ROK recon platoon that was mostly former guerillas who fought the Japanese and the Chinese Reds. The way it worked was Eli would light a bonfire a half-mile or so to our rear and dance around it...he was some sort of medicine man, I was told...and that dog would howl up a storm. The Chinese would get curious, and the snipers would pick 'em off.

Q: Yessir. What happened to the dog?

A: Same as the rest of 'em: their handlers had to put them out of their misery. Too *cold*, I was told. We buried 'em there off that little trail that wasn't on the maps.

Q: In North Korea?

A: Yup. Got the map coordinates in my files somewhere. I kept a running log of that goddamn disaster as it was happening because the unit's records got burned up. Soder used them for his bonfires before we got to the coast...

From the office of the Tribal President, December 197-

[T]he dogs would have been and still would be, considered members of the tribe. There's not much distinction made between animals and people in the Apache culture, especially if both have names. The spirit is what matters...

Fragment of Regimental diary, 90th Infantry Regiment, dated 28 November 1950

Master Sergeant Long Ears, SN K9...Sergeant Blue, SN K9...Corporal Ready, SN K9...died of wounds 0915. Buried at grid coordinates.....screen temperature -25 F, weather cloudy, occasional snow. Continuing southeasterly movement of column...125 effectives in TF, 67 wounded...Chinese activity during the day almost nil...S. African Mustangs flying CAP most of the time...night sniping activity by Det. I considered a major factor in the continued success of withdrawal...

From a letter from Leonard Billingsgate, author of Serving Many Masters: Dogs and Horses in the US Army 1917-45, *dated 29 February 197-*

If Long Ears was a Master Sergeant in Korea, he was either *very* old or *very* good at what he did. Sentinel dogs didn't rise above Sergeant First Class (that's three stripes and two rockers) before retirement. The trackers were something new in WWII, though, so they may have done some things with them that they didn't do with the sentinels and haven't done since.

My research on Long Ears has him a sergeant first class in '45 when he and Eli were mustered out. The dog *should* have been destroyed in Italy, but the tribe paid for his quarantine and his return. Not *unheard* of, but a bit unusual, since he was the only one of twenty dogs the tribe had with the detachment at the end of the war...

From a letter from Bart Nathaniel, archivist at the American Kennel Club, dated 17 May 197-

I was intrigued by your inquiry and did some checking. A bloodhound later named Long Ears was whelped in May 1935, the second of four males and two females by Tiger 6 Nast out of Patricia Ells 3 at Lebensborn Kennels in Detroit. The litters of two national champions, regardless of breed, are sold well in advance of whelping. One male was sold to the Apache Nation in Arizona. This dog was never registered with AKC.

This litter had all the makings of true champions. Some of Long Ears' siblings did indeed win and win big in national and international trials. Long Ears is the only one that did not compete but spent his life as a working dog.

Excerpt from an article published in Dog Fancier Magazine, *December 197-*

...And so to this day, the purebred bloodhound known as Long Ears, famous in law enforcement in two hemispheres, is buried somewhere in North Korea, and his master waits to rest with him.

Memo from Governor Long, 18 March 197-

To: Staff

From: RGL

Re: Eli Soder, Chief of Police of the Apache Nation

A few years ago, there was some concern about Chief Soder's health. Is this still a concern? Should we be looking for a new chief?

Fragment of a letter from George Thornton, dated 1 April 197-

I read your article in one of those in-flight magazines—and a little different version in *Reader's Digest*. I'm sure that you were talking about the column my old outfit in Korea joined up with in the winter of '50...I was an engineer. I blasted out three holes to put those dogs into...not one hole, but three...used mortar shells the ground was so hard...always wondered if they didn't get dug up and eaten...

Fragment of NSA intercept, Mainland Asia desk, dated 20 May 197-

...The articles spoke of the last column to leave North Korea from the lower Chongchon Valley. The writers are concerned with the life, death, and burial of one dog. The area they reference is untraveled and uninhabitable; there were no *Immun Gun* unit movements through it. Which Chinese units may have passed through coordinates....?

Excerpt from a letter to Senator Goldwater, dated 4 June 197-

...Chief Soder, whose health is failing, has rendered such remarkable service to the State and to the nation as a whole. The Apache Nation asks for a petition to the North Korean Government to consider the return of Long Ears' remains...

Excerpt from a letter from the Albanian Embassy to the Tribal President, received 5 June 197-

In light of your culture's attachment to the animals, the government of the Democratic People's Republic of Korea wishes to extend its services to assist the return of the animal's remains to its native soil...

Excerpt from a memo from American Delegation to the Peace Commission, Korean Demilitarized Zone, dated 7 September 197-

...Trouble is we've never asked the NK for the return of the dead (they send over one or two a year), even if we have a good idea where they might be. It raises a tricky issue...

Another problem is cultural: it's a *dog* we're talking about. We regard dogs as friends and companions, even part of the family. Koreans regard dogs as a part of the menu: dog meat is considered a delicacy...

Excerpt from a taped interview with H. Benton Philips from 30 October 197-

Q: So, what was your job with the 90th?

A: I was the S-2—Intelligence officer. I grew up in Japan and spoke Japanese and a little Korean and Mandarin Chinese, but my Army training was in intelligence.

Q: And were you with them in November and December of '50?

A: Certainly was. Joined the regiment about two days before the shit hit the fan, and the Chinese hit us. I was standing next to the Regimental commander when he got it. Couldn't have happened to a *nicer* arrogant *bastard*. He hung on for another two days, and we buried him at sea.

Q: How much contact did you have with Detachment I?

A: Well, they were HHC security, and they did send out patrols, so I debriefed them and interrogated their prisoners, along with Major Chin—my ROK counterpart—as long as he was around, and with Captain Yeoung, who was...well, he *was* in the ROK Army, but that *wasn't* his first allegiance...

Q: Did you have any contact with the tail detail at night?

A: You know about that? Huh. Been digging around a bit, eh?

Q: Yessir.

A: Most nights, I did. Me and Sergeant Griswold would hang out in the middle range—between the snipers and the fire—just to see if someone dropped we could get to for intel. Happened a couple times.

Q: Any idea what happened to Long Ears?

A: Eli's dog? Yeah. Eli and Dingy—he was a South African NCO who danced around the fire when Eli took breathers—shot him. They're the only two that really know, I guess. Eli never *said,* and Dingy—his full name is Dingeswaya—barely spoke. Poor beasts were suffering in that cold.

Q: As you recall, were they buried deep enough so that they wouldn't be dug up? Pretty desperate for food in North Korea back then.

A: Well, where we planted 'em was in this little cul-de-sac on the map, only it was just a loop away from the main road. Just the *maps* said it was a cul-de-sac. But I don't think that them being dug up is a big concern...

Q: Why not?

A: The reason the map is wrong. There were a monastery and hospital at the top of the rise that they used as a madhouse. Asians call it a place of rats. *Strong* spirits, *evil* spirits, live there, they believe. So does every other unwanted element in Asian society: the mad, the retarded, lepers, those with birth defects, cleft palates, and victims of all that sort of thing that aren't killed outright. Even the blind and those with burgundy wine stain rashes. *No* Korean or Chinese followed us through that valley because they were more afraid of those demons than they were of us getting out...

Q: Even the "godless" communists?

A: In Asia outside the cities, communism isn't as much a *religion* as it is in Europe; it's political affiliation. Peasants still talk about the spirits and gods and appeasing them, then wave Mao's little red book around...

From Dr. Davis Monthan, D.V.M., Chief of Canine Studies, University of Maryland Veterinary College, received 5 December 197-

If what we're talking about here is American Bloodhounds, I can understand why they suffered enough to be destroyed in that intense cold. Consider this: A cat has a sense of smell about three hundred times more sensitive than a human, and a dog about three hundred times *more* sensitive than a cat. But a bloodhound has a sense of smell so overdeveloped that it's probably 600 times more sensitive than *another* dog. Their olfactory acuity is rivaled in the animal world only by the shark. In cold *that* intense, the mucus membranes in their sinus cavities would have turned to solid ice. Without the ability to smell, they couldn't communicate, drink, eat, even relieve themselves. Any dog suffers in that environment to some extent, but bloodhounds *die* in it...

From the Soder file in Governor Long's office, dated 5 March 197-

...[B]ut he seems to have recovered. Unlike most of the Apache, Soder has never touched alcohol in his life. He has lived apart from those of his people who do drink. Still, he performs ceremonies as a shaman for his band. The men in his family are extraordinarily long-lived: his grandfather lived to

104, and his father is still going strong at nearly eighty..."

Minutes of the 3,4__plenary session of the Panmunjom Peace Conference, October 22, 197-

Agenda item US 45-7: The return of the remains of a dog known as Long Ears. The NK delegation took note of the request from the US. Asked why this would be important, US delegate SODER replied that it was important in Native American religion that souls rest together near their birthplace. No further comment from the NK delegation on this agenda item.

Fragment of NSA intercept, Mainland Asia department, a wireless telegraphic interception at 1623 hours October 23, 197-

...[T]he general sense was that this request is some sort of trick, though its nature is not clear. We suggest that someone go to the map coordinates and see if there isn't *some* truth to the story. But it seems very strange...

Fragment of intercept from USAF wireless communication originating in northern east Korea, November 197-

The region is inaccessible by all mechanized transport until at least mid-May...

Memo from the Historical Department, General Staff Division, Chinese People's Liberation Army, dated December 197-

In response to your inquiry: Of the PVA Fourth Army Group units in the vicinity, we can verify that two small divisions. The 91st (6,000 men) and 119th (ca 7,500 men) were in continuous contact with the rearguard unit south of the Chongchon, known as the 90th Regiment. It is suspected that this was a deception unit since it did not exist before the American intervention in Korea began and was not reconstituted after its destruction. Contact was lost only when it was evacuated off the western coast. Daylight casualties were severe due to extremely accurate bombing and strafing by aircraft. Nightly losses unacceptably high (over 100 per night). It was suspected that as a high-altitude radar device was targeting rally points, subsequent research has indicated the presence of infrared aiming devices, unknown to us at that time, in the hands of highly experienced marksmen. No similar incidents were known in the PVA before or after.

Fragment of a telephonic intercept from Prof. Hiram Gates, Professor of American Studies, Univ. of Calgary, Dated January 198-

Gates: Well, this is an Apache, then?

Unknown Voice: Yes, apparently.

G: All right. The Apache are Plains Indians. They are essentially monotheistic, but with flavorings that smack of Shinto ancestor worship. They didn't take to the idea of reservations well. Nor did they get along with their other Native American neighbors, the Cheyenne or Ute, at all until the white man showed up.

UV: But does this request make any sense culturally?

G: They see the spirit—life force if you will—as being a continuous existence. The only two states identifiable are this world and the spirit world, separated by the mysterious state of death. Over the hundreds of years of warfare with their neighbors, life and death had to start looking pretty much the same because they just didn't truck with the idea of multiple spirits. Being buried with the dog would make sense in their faith, yes, since it was a spiritual member of the tribe...

Intercept from NSA (CLASSIFIED), January 198-

...Your response is unacceptable. The beast was buried in that area in the worst winter on record in 1950, and the road has been improved since then. We demand that you go up there and find what you can...

Intercept form USAF wireless monitoring originating somewhere in northeastern Asia, February 198-

...Suppose this is a fact (and there is a growing body of evidence in its favor), and it appears to be culturally significant to an oppressed minority in America. In that case, there may be an unprecedented propaganda opportunity. If we could persuade the Americans to recognize the Apaches as sovereign, imagine what a precedent this may set for liberation movements in Africa and Asia, and even in the Americas...Even the Irish could take advantage...

Partial intercept from (TOP SECRET) originating from Mikoniev Academy of History near Moscow, decoded March 198-

...[T]he unit did indeed exist, though only for a short time as it was a sop to a wealthy American family. That it got to Korea seems to have been both a surprise and an embarrassment to the US Army since the regiment was very small and had never trained up for combat. It was thought to be a safe position but ultimately ended up protecting the entire XI US Corps' western flank after II ROK corps collapsed.

We have some evidence that the man Soder, a staff sergeant at the time, was present with the HHC and assigned a dog named Long Ears. Whether it was the same Long Ears as he had during our Fatherland War is unknown, but one of our assets did hear of the man Soder, who is now a decorated senior policeman in America, speak at an award banquet some years ago mention that he "wanted to rest with Long Ears," but there is no elaboration. Soder has been approached by Soviet assets but has resisted all recruitment attempts and appears to be unapproachable.

The man Soder has done a service for the Soviet Union nonetheless. One of the women killed in 1944 by a criminal called the Cairo Ripper was born in Ukraine and, as a prostitute, provided information collected from indiscrete British officers. Soder caught this Ripper, and he was brought to justice. The dog, Long Ears, also participated in this manhunt...

A partial intercept from USAF voice wireless monitoring (AM)

originating from 75 km NE of Pyongyang, on or about March 19th, 198-
...the remains of at least two canines were identified...both skulls found were shot in the head. Identity tags found with the remains are consistent with American pattern ID tags...

Excerpt from as a letter from George Strongman, received 15 April 198-
I saw you on the TV talking about Eli and Long Ears. I thought you might like to know. I was with Detachment I on the Chongchon; I was one of the night spotters. The first two nights on our withdrawal Eli sang harvest songs. That third night he changed to funeral songs and dances for the dead. *Those* went on for the next three nights as if mourning a great chief...

Address to the UN General Assembly by Thomas Soder, LTC, USA, 1 June 198-
The government of North Korea agrees to return the remains of my father's dog, but only to a sovereign Apache Nation recognized by this body. I realize that this would create significant difficulties politically between the United States and Mexico. Further, several other countries since aboriginal peoples have never been recognized as sovereign, but I must ask. This is the only thing that my father asked of his country or those other nations he has served. My father has served the United States, Mexico, Great Britain, the Republic of Korea, and his fellow Apaches for over sixty years. Can you find a way to recognize Apache sovereignty and its ancient boundaries on both sides of the US/Mexico border? Can my father finally rest in the land of his ancestors, accompanied by his faithful friend, in a manner befitting his religion?

Excerpt of an address delivered to the United Nations General Assembly by Dingeswaya, Paramount Chief of the Kwa-Zulu Nation, speaking on behalf of the Republic of South Africa, 199-
It is the Republic of South Africa's position, *and* the Leopard Throne's desire, that the state of Apacheria should be given the full support of this body as a symbol of the struggles of all indigenous peoples. This is the last service I can perform for my old comrade in arms.

Transcript of the fifteenth plenary session of the US/Mexico Committee on Apacheria, 11 September, 200-
Ambassador WILSON: On the US side, we're talking about six semi-permanent residents in twelve hundred square acres.

Ambassador RENDOVA: On the Mexican, *five* residents in *about* the same area. So, eleven people. For a man and his dog, we are granting sovereignty from both Mexico and the US? What sort of law enforcement will that part of the world have?

Consul MERCADO: They will be sovereign to the UN in *appearance* and allow law enforcement from Mexico and the US up to the borders.

WILSON: Will North Korea believe in such a sham being "sovereign?"

Consul IRVINE: Real question is, will the UN?

RENDOVA: Believe me, if they call Afghanistan and Somalia "sovereign," they'll call *anything* "sovereign."

Fragment of a press release from the Democratic People's Republic of Korea, 25 December 201-

…[G]iven the growing cooperation between our peoples in the strategic security of the Korean Peninsula, the Democratic People's Republic of Korea will release the remains of the *soldier* known as Long Ears to the Special Ambassador from the Republic of Apacheria, Thomas Soder…

News report from the Arizona Republic, *9 April 201-*

Fifteen years after his death, Chief Eli Soder was finally reunited yesterday with his beloved dog, Long Ears, in a private ceremony in the southern portion of the Apache reservation in Arizona called Apacheria. Also attending was the Ambassador from the Republic of South Africa, the *charge d'affairs* from the Republic of South Korea, and the chief's surviving children, Alice, Thomas, Henry, Adam, Sophia, and George.

What Happened

What happens to the battlefield after *the shooting's over?*

The waves washed the sand gently, rising and falling in an ageless rhythm. Three men stood on the landing craft's lowered ramp, slowly rolling with the sea, watching the beach. The sounds of battle on the mountains and valleys of the island were soft, muffled. Occasionally a string of tracers or an artillery explosion lit the verdant green of the jungle far inland.

A stream of boats wallowed and skittered in and out of another beach, off to the left, burying the yellow sand and white coral with crates and cans and supplies. The loudest noise heard by those in the landing craft was the grinding of bulldozer blades scraping off sand and coral, building a pier out into the ocean.

"Right here, Commander Jessup," the Marine lieutenant pointed out on the map, a bead of sweat dropping off his nose, shivering with fever. "Off to the right."

"Yes, I've *seen* it on the map, son. Now let me survey it in person, please." The lieutenant, tired and sick with pneumonia and a concussion, leaned on the side of the boat.

"Ain't his fault, skipper," the ensign whispered to Jessup. "He just went in where they dropped him."

"I know, Max, I know," Jessup said, squinting under the unrelenting tropical sun. "But, I have to figure out what happened." Dwight Jessup had been a homicide detective and a lieutenant in the Naval Reserve in Detroit before Pearl Harbor, and Ensign Maximillian Preble had been an insurance investigator and a part-time college student studying for the law. Now they spent their time trying to put together the puzzles of battles, figuring out who should be given medals and who courts-martialed. They had spent the day before in the hospital ships and the transports, interviewing *this* debacle's survivors. Now they were going to have a first-hand look at the battlefield.

The boat swerved, water splashing up on the ramp, and the two officers staggered briefly. "The reef," the coxswain shouted down. "Rip our bottom out." Jessup faced the shore as the boat turned parallel with the beach. He thought dimly about the coral reef, the reef that's *not* in front of the *right* beach. Eddies over the living fence mocked the craft as it slid by. Hulks of stranded landing craft dotted the exposed coral.

They turned again towards the shore, easing through the hole the Marines found through the reef by chance. The sunken Sherman's hatch stood open, water rushing and gurgling through the interior. *Sounds more like a sewer after a rainstorm than a tomb*, Jessup thought. As they neared the beach, they saw other landing craft in the cove. Some of the boats were floating, operating; many were not. The coxswain steered through the path marked by buoys and poles. The LCI, stranded in the high tide, sat at the far end.

Their landing craft ground in, ramp scraping loudly on the sand. "Ike Jessup," the commander said to a gaunt fatigue-clad figure meeting him as he and his survey party stepped off the ramp. "You're Beachmaster Findlay?"

"Yeah," the beachmaster said dully, "Burt Findlay. You're the headhunter from staff."

"After-action team. I just need to know what happened."

Findlay stared at him, disbelieving. "Yeah. Me too."

"When did *you* get called in," Jessup asked, flipping open a notebook.

"It was nearly noon on D-day before they realized there was no beach party here, but there were troops. I was the assistant on Green Two, and they told me to grab half our team and come over here."

"I see," Jessup nodded, feeling the sweat running down his spine and the blazing sun on his neck. "Pretty quiet down at the Green sector by then, wasn't it?"

"Yeah," Findlay sighed. "By the time I got *here*, it was pretty quiet too. Like most graveyards." He gazed around him with red-rimmed eyes. "I was in New Guinea for two years and a half-dozen beaches, and I never saw anything like *this*..."

"You know anything about the right side guide boat from Green Two, sir," Preble interrupted. "We still can't find either of them."

Findlay pointed his chin out to the sea. "One's out there on the reef, burned to the keel. It got separated from the first wave, and nobody ever heard from them again."

"Any survivors *at all* from the first wave?"

"Not *here*. *They* hit the *right* beach."

Jessup watched Findlay sidelong as the beachmaster's stubbled jaw worked a wad of tobacco. "What'd you do before the war, Commander?"

Findlay looked at him blankly. "Electrical engineer in St. Louis. You?"

"This. Ask a lot of questions, look for answers. Well, we'll look around for a while." Findlay watched Jessup and Preble walk up the beach between the engineer's swept-lane markers and white cotton tape, the sand yielding to their low shoes. They walked carefully around the wreckage and equipment. Japanese bodies, bloated and stinking, had lost their thin covering of sand that the beach party had tossed over them and were swarming with flies.

Jessup held his hand over his brow, scanning the low bluffs. Trunks of trees denuded by concussion and shrapnel poked the azure sky with a backdrop of green-carpeted mountains. The three coconut log bunkers built into the bluffs were just blackened hulks staring out to sea. Just below the pile was a pack howitzer behind a small dune, a scattering of empty shell casings around it.

"Mr. Preble," Jessup said, "I want some good shots of this. I want some from that gun, and I want some from each of the bunkers up there. Stowe," Jessup called out to his chief cartographer-surveyor bringing up the rear, "as soon as you get the locations recorded, let the beach party start cleaning up."

"Aye, sir," the chief called back, not looking up from his sketches, eyes tearing in the stench and heat. A rating got busy setting the transit tripod, leveling the instrument. Two photographers started clicking away, recording each frame in small notebooks, their blue shirts stained black with sweat. A young chief, whose films of the aftermath of the Pearl Harbor attacks were still classified, started setting up a movie camera.

The Marine lieutenant had followed Jessup, not looking at the carnage. He held his head high, staring above the horizon, not speaking. "Lieutenant, where did you come in?"

The Marine stared at Jessup, not comprehending. "Sir?"

"I said; where did *you* come in," the commander repeated gently, quietly. "Where did you hit the beach?"

The lieutenant looked around for a moment and raised his arm slowly, pointing down the shoreline. "Up there, where the beach starts to bend."

"OK. Let's go have a look." The lieutenant followed Jessup in a daze, stumbling in the soft sand, his fever raging. They walked past smashed weapons, rusting boxes littering the sand. Behind them, someone choked and gagged. *Keep a lid on, Ike. Just keep a lid on for another few minutes...*

They stood near the water's edge, looking out at the sea. "My boat grounded right straight out there," the lieutenant pointed, "and the coxswain dropped the ramp. We stepped out into chest-deep water and machine-gun fire from the left bunker. Half my platoon was dead before they got off the boat."

Jessup followed with his eyes, the light green water of the cove at the reef giving way to blue, then became transparent near the shore. He watched a bit of a map case floating on the rising waves, still dutifully strapped to the neck of its owner face-down and half-buried on the beach near his feet. Jessup bent, felt for dog tags, waved away the swarming flies, and fought back a rising tide of nausea. *Map case means officer...*

"Captain Grissom," the lieutenant said. "King company commander. He was in my boat." Jessup watched the Marine out of the corner of his eye, trying not to think about the clammy, tight skin his hand found. "Colonel

Nelson, the battalion commander, went in on the *right* beach. After Grissom got it, they *say* I was the senior officer on *this* beach. But I was out on the reef excuse me, sir...." he bolted up the beach, dropped to his knees, and retched.

Two Marines sauntered up to Jessup in the nonchalant, worn air of senior NCOs compelled to talk to officers they didn't know, their rifles slung over their shoulders. "Sergeant Lathrup, sir," the first said, a cinnamon-haired, grizzled veteran of twenty-two with eyes much older. "We're to report to you."

Jessup consulted his notebook briefly. "George Company, second wave, right?"

"Yessir."

"And you must be..."

"Sergeant Sikorski, sir. How Company." Sikorski had patches of gray in his coal-black beard, an old man at twenty-three.

"*Third* wave, yes. Did either of you *see* a guide boat on the way in?" The two Marines looked at each other, shaking their heads.

"I thought *that* was kinda funny, sir," Sikorski said, the senior of the two by at least one island. "I was on the right flank in the first wave on Red On at Tarawa, and the guide boat took us all the way to the reef. Never saw one *here*, though."

"Did you say anything to anybody?"

"Well, sir, the boat crew was kinda busy at the time, what with that Jap howitzer hittin' us and the cross-current pushing us along. I figured they knew where they were goin'...."

"What struck me at the time, though," Lathrup interrupted, "was all the smoke off the beach. I mean, the major bombardment had ended, and, well, where'd all the smoke come from, anyway? The boat waves were all mixed up, and the only reference I could see was the transport we'd come from. I didn't see the beach until just before we dropped the ramp right up there on the left end of the cove..."

"Oh," Jessup said, "so it was *your* boat group that found the hole in the reef?"

"Yeah, I guess. *Our* boats went right in..."

"Fire in the hole," someone yelled, and Jessup bent over at the explosion near the water's edge. A fountain of mud and water rose in the clear sky, falling sloppily back to earth. The Marines watched calmly.

"What was *that*," Jessup shouted, slightly annoyed.

"Five-inch dud," came the reply, with an added "sir," just in case.

"...And we started gettin' off," Lathrup continued. "That's most of the First Platoon," he pointed down the beach at the wreckage in front of the left bunker. "Japs waited until they were right in front. Didn't stand a chance."

He watched the place briefly as if waiting for the Marines to get up again.

"How about you, Sikorski?"

"*Right* flank. We went into the reef. The boat with the Skipper—Captain Albright—got it from that antitank gun right away, went through, and went off on the engine. Nobody got off his boat in one piece." Sikorski watched the reef, the flecks of white foam on the coral, and shells of landing craft stranded on it.

"Who marked the hole?"

"Well," Lathrup drawled, "once I got ashore, I could see we were the only ones still dry, and our boat group was pulling out, so I sent Corporal Jacust back with some range markers to find the edge. *He* got it, so I sent Sergeant Moll. *He* got it, and then the tank lighter came in and ground on the reef..."

"We saw that," Sikorski interrupted, "so our Lieutenant—that's him up there, puking—waded back out, yanked a jackstaff off one of the boats, and walked across the reef. All the way across...that's, what, a thousand yards, and didn't get a scratch on him."

"Yeah," Lathrup said dully. "Too late for them tankers, though. I dunno what them yahoos was thinkin', but droppin' the ramp *that* far out...*Shit*," he finished, visibly disgusted.

"Who brought that howitzer in?"

"Oh," Lathrup said, looking back to the gun. "*That* was French Jack... um, no. Corporal Jacques D'Estaing. We called him "French Jack" because he *was* French. He claimed he jumped ship when the Japs occupied Haiphong. Anyways, he joined the Marines in New Caledonia, but I'll be damned if I know how he got there. He told the story a hundred times, and no two were alike. Guess we'll never really know now." He went glass-eyed, staring at the bullet-scarred gun, voice soft. "His boat grounded on the reef out there, and he staggered in with that damn gun tube on his back. More guys went out for the rest of the gun, and they keep gettin' killed. D'Estaing fires the first round from the sand, the second from just the trails when he got that left bunker. He got the third round off with the wheels on. We had this chain of guys all the way back to that damn boat out on the reef, handin' ammo, and parts in. They kept gettin' killed, but we kept fillin' in the holes. Finally, he got that center bunker up there. Then, that right bunker, over there, *they* got *him*." Lathrup stared the hollow, lifeless stare of a dead man watching the living, a thousand-yard stare that spoke of horror and weariness. Sikorski batted Lathrup lightly on the shoulder and stuck a lit cigarette in his mouth. Lathrup looked at his comrade briefly, snarled "Semper *Fi*, Mac," and took a drag.

A rattle of gunfire reached the beach, and both looked up at the jungle. "Is that all, sir?" They were staring at the green wall of foliage, listening carefully to the battle still raging inland.

"Just one more thing," Jessup said, watching them. "How many men are in your companies now?"

"We embarked two hundred fifty, counting the engineer platoon," Lathrup said, a Marine again. "This mornin's report showed fifty-five present for duty."

"A hundred ninety embarked," Sikorski reported just as crisply. "Thirty-one present for duty this morning."

"All right," Jessup told them. "Go back to your units. I may want to talk to you again." The two NCOs nodded quickly and turned away. Jessup started to salute, remembered the tactical SOP forbade it, and let them go.

Jesus, Jessup thought, unable to imagine saying much else, even to himself. Preble waved at him from in front of the center bunker some fifty yards up the beach. The higher Jessup walked, the firmer the sand was until it was crusty-hard near Preble and the two bluejackets he was with. The heat reflected brutally off the baked sand, radiating through his shoes until he thought his feet would burn. "You'll *want* to talk to these guys," Preble said, a hint of triumph in his voice.

"Kolmana, sir," the beefy Hawaiian with an arm in a sling said, coming wearily to his feet. "Brocks, sir," the blonde, skinny kid with a bandaged foot said, coming to a slightly slower attention.

"As you were, boys, as you were," Jessup told them lightly. They sat down again on the log parapet. Behind them were the remains of a small Japanese squad, weapons at the ready, burned to a crisp.

"Quartermaster Second Class Kolmana was by the helm of the LCI," Preble explained. "Gunner's Mate First Class Brocks was on the bow gun."

"I was told the crew was all killed or on a hospital ship," Jessup blurted eagerly.

"We stayed behind with Mr. Keen, sir," Kolmana said. "All the rest were worse off than us."

"Who's Mr. Keen?"

"He's the exec, or I guess he's skipper now, now that Mr. Spitzer's dead."

What a break! Actual eyeball witnesses to that damnfool run into the beach who weren't saved by it. Christ, you'd think that damn thing was helmed by Superman to hear some of those Marines talk about it. "OK, Kolmana; you first. What did you do before you came over to the cove here?"

"We'd just cleared off our beach—Red Three, a thousand yards up—and headed back for the transport serea. That Jap gun out on the peninsula wasn't shootin' at us anymore."

"Yes. The destroyers finally found it," Jessup offered. "Why did you go back to shore without orders from the transport commander?" *Was Spitzer out of his Goddamn mind?*

"I think it was because the first beach party for Red Two—that's what *this* was supposed to be, only a thousand yards down *that* way—got mostly killed, and we picked up a raft from one of their boats. The skipper decided that since they hit the wrong beach and didn't seem to have a beach party, they might need a hand clearing off. The radios were on the fritz again, and we were behind a smoke cloud, so we couldn't see any visual signals, let alone make any, and we weren't quite sure where *out* was, so we went back in. What made all the smoke, sir?"

"One of the destroyers hit an old latex dump with a star shell when they were trying to find that gun," Preble mumbled quietly. "Where was everybody on the LCI when you headed back in?"

"Well, sir, I was on the annunciator by the helm, Quartermaster First Gutteriez was on the wheel, and the skipper was up on the bridge, that's all I know was anywhere."

"OK. Go on," Jessup said.

"We head into the beach and see this cove. By then, we've taken on about a hundred guys from three waves, and there's still guys in the water hollering for help, and the props just about got fouled from all the bodies and junk in the drink, and we started taking fire from right over there," he pointed at the right bunker.

"OK," Jessup said absently, studying the torn and mangled log structure from above its killing arc for the first time. *Looks innocent now.* "Then what?"

"Well, the first hit we got killed the skipper. I was right next to the voice tube, so I can hear all this. Then the next one came into the wheelhouse where I was, got Gutteriez in the head, and I got a splinter or two, and then we get hit from tracers, and there was a fire below. I hollered about I was alone in there, and the next I know, Mr. Keen is in there with me on the wheel, yellin' at me to stay put. He says the skipper was hurt bad, and he was taking the conn, and we're headed in."

"What about *you*," Jessup asked Brocks. "Where were *you*?"

"Up forward on my gun. One hit killed the ammo passers below and cut off the hoist. I thought we were headed out, but we got hit some more, and we kept goin' in. Right about then, the Chief jumped up into the tub..."

"CPO Winters," Preble said.

"Yessir, and he says the only chance of savin' the boat was to beach her, and we were such a big target we had to get in real close and get that Jap bunker.

"Well, we pass by a Gyrene standin' out in the water wavin' a pole over his head, and then we heeled over to starboard faster'n I thought we *could*..."

"Yeah," Kolmana broke in, "Mr. Keen jerked the wheel over and told me to jam the port engine forward and the starboard back. That big gun and them heavy machine guns was tearing us up, and we was just covered with splinters, and the engine room was hollering about a fire in the propeller shaft housing and water coming in, and the bow gun shield fell off..."

"Naw," Brocks answered, as if to the village idiot. "The Chief cut it off with a torch. It was keepin' us from depressin' the gun. That damn shield came off, and a second later, so did the Chief's head and the gun captain's legs..."

"How'd you keep up ammo with the chute cut off?"

"The guys in the well formed a line and passed it forward from the after gun. Gillespie—one of the second loaders—reached back and kept passin' it in even after his right arm got cut off and he tied his belt to it, and Calloran kept on trainin' us even after he got a splinter through both lungs. Bittich was the last first loader left by the time we hit the sand, standin' between them hot tubes, skin and hair burnin' off and stinkin' to high heaven ..."

"What happened after you hit the beach?"

"Well, sir, not much else. We fired at that damn bunker 'till it didn't shoot no more, and the guys in the well got out and made sure with a bunch of grenades. That's all there *was*, really."

That's all there was. Jessup distractedly scratched some notes. *That's all there was...* "What was your gun station?"

"Pointer, sir. I stomped the trigger all the way in." Jessup scratched more notes, wondering if *any* of this was going to be believed.

His reverie was interrupted by Beachmaster Findlay, who'd listened to a good part of the story. "Commander Jessup, the chaplains and graves people want to start to clean up..."

Jessup looked around the beach, the engineers with their mine detectors marking swept lanes, corpsmen checking unmarked bodies for signs of life. "Well, Mr. Preble, do we have enough?"

"I think so, sir," Preble answered. "Chief Stowe," he shouted to the survey party, "Let 'em clean up?" Stowe waved assent. "Just leave the Jap equipment for a while. Intelligence will want to see it in context."

"All right, Commander," Jessup sighed.

"Thanks." Findlay staggered off, donning a gauze mask.

Jessup watched after him. "You'd better get back aboard," he told the sailors. "It's going to get mighty foul out here when they start moving the dead." The sailors ambled back to their battered landing craft; Brocks hobbling on his good leg and leaning on Kolmana, who took up the weight without complaint.

"Let's get outta here, Max," Jessup said. "We'll come back later if we have to."

Findlay met them as they headed back down to the sea. The cleanup crew had begun to move the bodies onto the canvas tarpaulins that served as shrouds. Findlay winced at the loud *thut* of a meathook as it dug into a breastbone nearby. "Commander Jessup," he said through his mask, "I want to recommend those sailors for Navy Crosses."

"I'll go you one better, Commander," Jessup replied. "I'm gonna put that LCI's skipper and that Lieutenant *and* that Marine gunner up for Congressionals and everybody else on this *cocked-up* beach up for Navy Crosses. You endorse the statements?"

"*Proud* to."

Jessup and Preble were nearly at their LCM when a naval officer in tattered khakis shouted at Jessup. "Ensign Keen, sir," the young officer reported. He flinched at a burst of small-arms fire that sounded uncomfortably close but, reflected on some mountain rock, was more than a mile away. "I was told to report to you."

"You're the skipper of the LCI," Jessup replied, extending his hand. "*Pleased* to meet you." His grip was loose, cold, wet.

"*LCI-578*, but I'm the *exec*, sir," the young man replied hurriedly, stumbling over words. "We call her the *Bayard*, "cause the village of Bayard, Indiana, bought her. Big bond drive they had, made a newsreel out of it." *Still hasn't quite got over it*, Jessup thought sadly. *Been in command of the most heroic vessel in these waters for two days, and he still calls himself the executive officer.* "They couldn't afford anything bigger, so the Navy let them buy an LCI. The Mayor and the City Council came out when she was launched."

"I'm sure they *did*, son," Jessup interrupted solicitously. "But I want to know *how* you brought that sinking vessel into the cove, avoided a coral reef, turned ninety degrees to the beach, and then ran in while dueling with an antitank gun. A duel you *won*, by the way."

Keen looked at Jessup, startled, and then looked at his craft, turning his back abruptly. Jessup moved to his side, gazed at the plywood and steel structure, the holes blown through her hull, upper works splintered, forward guns and ramps spattered with the blood of her gun crews and chain of ammo handlers, the flag still flying from her mast.

"We *did* all that," Keen muttered quizzically, surveying the carnage of his vessel. A landing craft motor revved up to clear the beach, piled high with canvas cocoons. The graves detail watched briefly changed their masks and gloves, grabbed up a bundle of canvas, and trudged up the beach again. "What I *remember* doesn't make sense," Keen continued dully, twisting his face into a scowl. "I can remember hearing the skipper was badly hurt, and then I remember somebody out in the water waving a pole. And then I remember thinking that they hadn't painted the inside of the wheelhouse lately, and I could see red lead. But that doesn't make sense because my battle station was forward in the cargo well.

"I...am...not...a...brave...man," he sputtered haltingly. "I was raised in the Amish tradition. I left that world and joined the Navy when my folks were killed by a hobo in '35. I wanted to find out what this vengeful God had made of the rest of the world." He turned away from his vessel and stared out at the sea. "I found out."

Was it God or man who made a boy barely old enough to shave hold a pole over his head for half a day up to his chest in the surf? Who made a refugee Frenchman brave withering fire to perform a feat of superhuman strength and courage under a foreign flag? Who made a spit-kit bought with Midwestern farmers' savings roar into hostile gunfire and sacrifice herself and her crew to save the WRONG beach?

"Yes," Jessup whispered, "He made *men*. And *men* make *mistakes*. And He made *other* men who have to *fix* the mistakes."

"And he made the sea," Keen muttered. "The all-forgiving sea..."

They watched the sea wash the sand in the merciless tropical sun, the eternal rhythmic water, erasing the traces of men's mistakes, and washing the beach clean again.

Buddies

The bonds forged between men in war are stronger than those between any other friends...

The young lieutenant slept on a litter. The older sergeant sat beside him on the stony beach shingle. The sergeant watched the wave-tossed, angry sea and the boats skittering in and out from the invasion armada offshore. He craned his neck at the swarms of black-and-white striped airplanes overhead.

The lieutenant had been his Ranger Buddy since they joined the platoon four months before. To the US Army Rangers, the buddy system was all-important. Your Ranger Buddy was your legs when yours had given out; your eyes when yours were tired. You shared your rations when they were short, your missions great and small, your tents wet and dry, and your money between paydays. You were a part of one another.

Behind them rose a hundred feet of sheer rock called Pointe du Hoc. Allied planners decided that the bunkers on top of the cliffs contained large coastal guns that could shoot up the D-Day landing forces. So in went the Rangers.

A moan rose from the litter. "Sir?" the sergeant asked, straining to hear over the din of the surf.

"Hello, Sergeant," the lieutenant answered softly, his speech thick from morphine. "How's the platoon?"

"Why, they're just fine, sir. Just fine," the sergeant replied cheerfully, not looking at him. "I just thought I'd keep you company until the medics evacuated you."

"That's very good of you, Sergeant, but you really should be with the men."

"They're in good hands, sir. Sergeant Westphal is in charge of them now. We're beach security, sir. You *do* remember that from the briefing, don't you, sir? The platoon has nothing to do for the time being."

"Yes, I remember, Sergeant." He was quiet again. His breathing was slow and shallow. A breeze picked up a part of a rope ladder on the cliff, battering it against a hollow rock. The sergeant turned and looked back at it, then back to the sea. "How did the platoon do, Sergeant? Did we get up the cliffs first?"

"Yessir, we *certainly* did," the sergeant answered, remembering the assault. The grappling hooks and ropes shooting up the cliffs, the grenades tumbling down, the near-vertical grazing fire that swept the wall, Rangers digging handholds in the rock face with bayonets. "We got up there in record time. We beat Easy Company's assault platoon by a full minute." *A full minute while we took out two machine guns with four guys. Four out of forty that were supposed to get up there. While the rest of the platoon and the whole of Baker Company were pinned down, we found a way up a crevice and came across the top like Gangbusters. We got up there, all right.*

"We got the guns then?"

"Yessir. We got the guns." *The guns weren't there. The bunkers were, but no guns.* "Mission accomplished, sir."

"That's good." Silence again. "How about casualties? Did we suffer many casualties?"

"*Not* bad, sir." *While our rope was climbing up the hidden crevice, three others were cut down or broke loose. Fifteen guys fell. Three got up again. And the Kraut machine guns sprayed the cliff face while we worked up the wall, hand-over-hand, on ropes and scaling ladders and fingerholds.* "There's McGivney; he's dead. Rodgers, too, I think. Kalen; he busted his skull. Pitts got a bullet in the shoulder. And *you*, sir." *And there's Krieger, who broke his neck. And Henderson was shot through the head. And Willie Smith got blown up by a grenade. And Charles got hung by barb wire when he slipped near the top. And Mitgang...*

"Yes. What do they *say* about me, anyway?"

"Oh, you'll be up and around in no time, sir." *The bullet that went into your shoulder from above you, sir, it made a mess of your liver. And then when you fell seventy feet or so, you broke your back, sir. But that wasn't enough, sir. Nossir, not for you. You had to survive all that—you, the All-American, the poster model for the Boy Next Door. But you won't stay long. The medics say no more than a couple hours.*

The lieutenant chuckled softly. "You're a good friend, Sergeant. But you're an awful liar."

"Yessir," the sergeant answered. "I'm a *lot* of things, sir. The Lieutenant knows me too well."

"I'm supposed to, Sergeant. Isn't that what being a Ranger Buddy is all for?" He moaned softly, catching his breath. "I wanted to thank you, Sergeant, for being my Ranger Buddy."

"No thanks needed, sir. Just doin' what I'm supposed to. Ranger Buddies is all about lookin' out for each other." *Get this over with, you poor kid.*

"I *want* to, anyway. I never did thank you for getting me out of that scrape at Anzio."

"Wasn't *just* you, sir."

"I know. It was me, Captain Beel, Major Stanley, the Colonel, a lot of us.

If it wasn't for *that...*"

"Never mind, sir." The sergeant lit two cigarettes and put one in the lieutenant's mouth. "That's just my job." A dull boom rolled across the water. *Down the beach. I thought we had troubles. Wonder what's goin' on down there?*

"Yeah," the lieutenant said softly. "But if it wasn't for *that*, we wouldn't have got to be friends."

"Well, sir, I think there's more *to* it than that..."

"And if *you* hadn't socked that Bobbie."

"Yessir," the sergeant chuckled, flicking the ash off the lieutenant's cigarette. "That got me busted back down to buck sergeant, and then you got moved outta staff when you bailed me out. But that damn Limey deserved it."

"I suppose," the lieutenant answered, coughing. "What'd he do?"

"Called us *damn foreigners. Us.* We come over here to get the Brits outta a jam, and we get called *damn foreigners.* But how was I supposed to know he was a cop?"

"And a Chief Inspector at that," the lieutenant whispered. Silence again. A bird squeaked and crackled as it flew across the beach, lighting on the cliffs behind them. "How did Millen do, Sergeant? He was so frightened."

"Who? Oh, Millen. Just fine, sir; just fine." *He led the charge across the cliff. When his rifle jammed, he started picking up Krauts and throwing them off the cliff. Funny how those real big guys get so scared...*

"That's good, Sergeant." The sergeant leaned over and removed the butt from the lieutenant's lips. "Is it dark, Sergeant? Is it night?"

"Yessir," the sergeant replied, looking up at the glowing white ball of the noon sun behind the overcast. "Night, sir."

"I'll be going soon, Sergeant," the lieutenant whispered. "Tell my folks I did what they asked me to do."

The sergeant remembered the boy's parents' picture he kept on his footlocker lid, storekeepers in Nebraska, looking brave for their eldest son. "I'll do that, sir."

"Mail my letters for me..."

Then, the picture of that girl: burnished copper hair and fresh-scrubbed freckles, a lacy white collar on a cornflower blue dress, and perfect white gloves. "Yessir."

"One more thing, Sergeant."

"Yessir?"

"*Where* are you from?"

"Why, the lieutenant knows I'm from the Army."

"You weren't *born* in the Army, Sergeant. You told me *that* much." The lieutenant smiled thinly. "Where *were* you born?"

The sergeant stared out at the sea. A vision of the cinder-colored baseball field next to his house came back to him. The last time he saw his father just before he ran off flashed in his mind: cauliflower ears and a broken nose from prizefighting, the young barmaid who was to be a new "mother." He had to imagine an older brother who he hadn't seen or heard from in ten years. He wondered vaguely how he might go about trying to find him. "I was born and raised in Pittsburgh, sir."

"Pittsburgh," the lieutenant coughed again. "About as far from this place as Grand Forks."

In more ways than one, sir. "Yessir."

"Take care of the men, Sergeant."

Of course, sir. I'll watch their asses and wipe their noses, crack their chops, censor their mail, and protect them from the yahoos called officers— present company excepted, sir—bent on getting them killed. "Yessir. Keep your powder dry and tomahawk sharp."

In a few minutes, the sergeant looked over at the lieutenant. His face was calm, his young eyes dull and steady. A fleck of mud on his check seemed somehow incongruous. The sergeant moistened a finger and rubbed off the offending spot. He closed the boy's eyes.

After some minutes, the sergeant stood up and started, slowly, walking away. He motioned to the chaplain's assistant on the other side of the rock spur, pointing behind him. "He's all yours, Mack."

The sergeant gradually gained speed and purpose. *The platoon needs everybody they can get.* "*Westphal*," he called in his familiar, gravel voice. "Let's get *back* in the war. How many we got left?"

"Countin' you an' me, fourteen."

We hit the beach with forty.

As they started climbing the rope ladders, one of the platoon's newer replacements nudged his old-hand buddy. "What's got into the Sarge?" he wondered aloud.

"*Nothin'*, rookie," the buddy replied. "*Nothin'* at all. Sarge just got some sand in his eyes, is all."

Nowhere To Be Found

Not every soldier has to fight the war from the front. And not every soldier carries a weapon...

It was the sand that Jack Masters couldn't get used to. Always seemed like there was sand in everything: underwear, socks, shoes, food. Though it was only midmorning, the sun had already boiled off the damp of the desert winter night and left the men stiff and the tents smelly.

Squinting against the unrelenting desert sun, he watched the figures bounce towards the field in the shimmering haze. They came from out of the nowhere of the Empty Place (as the Bedouins called the depths of the Nefud Desert) to the nowhere of Masters' Wadi Jamblatt emergency airfield.

Doctor Julius Bulow waited with Masters. Bulow was an Austrian-born missionary to the Bedouins of the central Arabian Desert and the six families of herders that lived at the water holes and sparse pasture of Wadi Jumblatt. After twenty years, he could not boast of a single *long-term* convert to Christianity (it displeased the *mullahs* and *imams*), but the *medical* portion of his mission was successful. Bulow also acted as translator, physician, and chaplain for the handful of Americans at the field. The horsemen drew near. "Sheik Fahad," Bulow said. "Salt caravan."

The riders in the lead found water and safe passage for the camel trains and flocks that followed. In this part of the world, salt was worth more than gold and far more than the poisonous black liquid the British and Americans wanted so badly. The Bedouins of Fahad's tribe traded salt mined in the deep desert pans for hard currency to buy manufactured goods.

Masters had met the big sheik of an empire of dust and wind, and an area larger than many states, with perhaps ten thousand people living on its rim. He and his men had been deposited at Wadi Jamblatt two years before, in a great rush of airbase-building before the North African invasion. Fahad was a haughty cuss, distantly related to the Saudi royal family, who eyed the American field in his caravan route as a curious annoyance, but was willing to put up with them as long as he and his people were left alone…and Bulow tended to their complaints from time to time. Masters traded weapons and ammunition for fresh food, salt, and information on weather and other tribes.

The horsemen galloped up and ground to a dusty halt ten yards away from

Masters and Bulow. "*Salaam Aleichem,*" Bulow called.

"*Aleichem Salaam,*" Fahad replied. That would be the only time he would be *expected* to talk to Bulow. Fahad was courteous to the missionary-doctor, but that was all.

Fahad dismounted and tossed his horses' reigns casually behind him. A retainer deftly caught them in midair. He walked stiffly towards Masters and Bulow with the stiff gait of an old man who'd spent a bit too long on horseback. He was dressed in traditional robes but wore finely tooled German boots and *feldgrau* trousers. Local legend held that he'd took them off a German he killed during the brief campaign in Syria when he took a small band there under British pay.

"*Salaam Aleichem,* Sheikh Fahad," Masters said. "I trust you are well."

Fahad regarded Masters blankly and then twisted into curiosity, then amusement. Masters had been told that Fahad put up with the Major's insulting familiarity only because he did it in Arabic. "*Aleichem Salaam,* Major. I am *most* well. Your tongue is *much* improved."

"*Thank* you, Sheikh Fahad, you are most kind. I offer the humble hospitality of my mess tent. Come, we shall drink coffee and celebrate the grace of Allah that has brought us back together again." Masters had learned to offer hospitality that all good Muslims must accept, and the tribesmen were usually happy to get the hard-to-get stimulant.

Masters positioned himself to the left and rear of Fahad and directed him to the mess tent. Bulow followed behind, and two of Fahad's retainers followed. Inside, a large carpet had been spread over the canvas floor, tables and chairs stacked at the far end. Cornwall, the cook, stood by with steaming coffee from the large urn. The three sat in a rough circle on the carpet while Cornwall gave them each a steel cup, set the serving tray on the floor, and backed away. They drank coffee in silence.

When Fahad's cup was empty, Masters spoke. "What brings you to Wadi Jumblatt, Sheikh?" The caravans usually bypassed Jumblatt on the journey, preferring the greener pastures further south.

Fahad's eyes flashed briefly at the breach of etiquette but then became calm. It was not for *anyone,* after all, to ask a sheik *his* business. "Ached," he called, and a retainer entered the tent. "*Show* them," he ordered. The boy produced a small sack and poured the contents on the carpet. A collection of eyeglasses, wallets, dog tags, watches, and rings tumbled on the carpet.

Masters eyed the pile carefully, watching Fahad out of the corner of an eye. The caravans sometimes found wrecks in the desert, returning the personal items for rewards. At least one ship went down every other month flying across Arabia. However, Fahad was a wealthy man (in relative terms), with a monopoly on the salt pans. *Why would he return this?*

Fahad gestured to the pile, inviting Masters to examine it. He dug in, looking for anything that might have a date. Inside a wallet was a laundry ticket dated only two weeks before. *This is recent.* "Had they been dead long," Masters asked guardedly.

"The one who was dead was killed when the machine fell," Fahad answered. "What will you pay for the *live* ones?"

Masters and Bulow stared at the chieftain, waiting. Bedouin humor was often quite black. "They are still *alive*," Bulow asked, incredulous.

Fahad answered without shifting his blank gaze from Masters. "Yes. *Five* of them still live. *How much* will you pay?"

"Hodges," Masters called out, hoping his First Sergeant was outside where he was supposed to be. "Bring me a case of Garands and a case of Colts." Then he replied to Fahad, keeping his voice as even as he could manage. "I will pay *one* case of rifles and *one* of pistols for every living American."

Surprised, Fahad grinned briefly and then held his cup high to be refilled. The retainer named Ached ladled. In a few minutes, the crates were dragged in. Fahad got up on his knees and opened the latches methodically. He removed a pistol, tested the trigger and cylinder, and replaced it in the case. He glanced at the rifles indifferently. "Cartridges?"

"Wait," Masters said. "*Where* are the Americans?" Fahad looked at Masters again, this time with a glimmer of admiration. Masters was *trying* to think like a trader.

"They are a day's journey away."

"*Where* did the machine fall?"

"*Three* day's journey. Allah favored us when we *saw* it come down."

"*Allahu Akbar. Blessed* is the name of Allah," Masters responded impatiently, surprising himself with the correct, polite response. "When can they be here?"

"If Allah and I *wish*, tonight," Fahad responded evenly, gesturing for more coffee. "*If* Allah and I *wish*."

"All right," Masters said. "A thousand cartridges for pistols and a thousand for rifles..."

"For *each* rifle and *each* pistol?"

"Yes, if you wish. If you will *wait* for the cartridges..."

"*I* can wait. Can *you*?"

"You barter for men's lives," Bulow shouted impolitely. "You'll trade human flesh for guns and bullets?"

"My father traded in slaves, Physician," Fahad replied, not looking at him. "When Allah takes a man to his bosom, our custom is to kill his slaves or free them. I have never wanted to own another man. I freed the slaves my father owned and own none myself. I deal *not* in flesh," Fahad finished, slightly amused. "*I* deal in *valuable* flesh."

"Yes. *Very* well," Masters said, keeping his voice as even as he could. "You shall have your guns and your cartridges by morning." *If they've gotta parachute 'em in, they will,* "I must contact my superiors."

"*Done*," Fahad shouted, extending his hand at Masters. Masters, slightly taken aback, took the callused hand. "We have a bargain," Fahad called, then said something unintelligible to Ached, who went out. "He will fetch your countrymen," Fahad sighed as he ladled himself more coffee. "But, you need *not* contact your superiors."

"Why?"

Fahad turned to Bulow, who started. "You have skill in healing arts, do you not?"

"Yes, I do," the priest answered, flabbergasted. "God has...*Allah* has... blessed me with some skills."

"And you are a priest of an infidel religion, are you not?"

"Yes. I am a priest of the Lutheran church, a Christian sect."

"Hmm," Fahad mused. "Your sects are *probably* as confusing as *ours*. This is the season when Christians celebrate the birth of Jesus, son of Miriam, the Nazarene you Christians call the Promised One, yes?"

"Yes. We call this season Christmas."

Fahad contemplated his coffee cup. He looked again at Bulow. "The Koran teaches that Jesus, son of Miriam, was the Messenger of Allah," Fahad muttered, furrowing his brow in thought. He returned his gaze to his coffee cup before he looked at Bulow again. "You healed my uncle years ago. He still lives."

"Allah is merciful..."

"Allah has had little to do with it, but Allah be praised," Fahad answered quietly. "Uncle has not left Riyadh in *years*." He studied Masters' and Bulow's faces. "This is a season for giving and receiving gifts, yes? The season for miracles?" Fahad's voice was firm but understated.

"Yes. A season for goodwill to all men," Masters ventured carefully.

"Is this what Jesus teaches you?" Fahad glanced at both men,

"Yes. This and that redemption of sin is possible for those of faith," Bulow answered.

"Ah, *yes*; faith." He was quiet again. He set down his coffee cup and looked at Bulow, his stare firm and unblinking, his wrists propped on his knees. Bulow vaguely thought of a judge about to pronounce a sentence. "I am Sheikh of the Nefud Bedouin," Fahad said, "lord of a land of scorpions and sand, but rich in salt. My tribe now numbers twice what my father ruled, *five times* what *his* father ruled. When we found the men from the flying machine, my tribe wanted a huge ransom. And now they think they will get one. But *I* want a ransom for *myself*." He paused, considering the reaction from both Masters and Bulow. Seeing nothing, he seemed satisfied. "I have seen fifty feasts of Ramadan, *five* more than my father saw. I have had three wives. Two of them have died, giving dead children birth. I have no son to inherit my tribe. My third wife is with child, and the midwives fear, for her time comes *now*. *I* fear, for there are few other suitable wives for me. I want a son, and I *want* my *wife* to *live*."

He looked hard at Bulow. "Can you give Nivan Gamaliel ibn Saud Fahad nur Muhammad Haj a living wife *and* living baby son? Will you have goodwill for a non-believer in your Promised One's divinity? Can you help Allah *make* a miracle in this season of miracles?"

Bulow was stunned. "I can but try."

• • •

The supply ship (a converted B-24 bomber) touched down on the runway and rolled to a stop. A joke among aircrews was that if you wanted to save your brakes, land at Wadi Jumblatt with its endless runway. Masters' men came out of their tents surprised, for the supply run wasn't due for another week. Masters waited outside the communications tent, surprised at the arrival but unwilling to leave Fahad, who was at prayers with his retainers not far away. His wife was in Bulow's hut on the other side of the field. The five survivors of the B-24 crash (dehydrated, dirty, tired, but otherwise none the worse for their experience) slept in the mess tent.

The evening shadows were long before the cargo was unloaded, which meant that the supply ship was stuck until dawn. The load was a little odd: Turkeys packed in dry ice, potatoes, spices for stuffing, cranberries in cans. Bulow's Lutheran sponsors had sent the bounty, insisting that it arrive before the holiday. And with it came a tree—a scrawny knee-high blue spruce, packed in wet earth and wrapped in burlap and rayon.

"Get that damn tree off my ship," the pilot cried. "Damn thing's been dropping needles all over since we left Marrakech."

"You guys came all the way from Marrakech?"

"Naw. Passaic, New Jersey. *One* cargo, *one* run. Loaded it on special for you guys. Orders from higher-up. And, we got orders *en route* to pick up your crash survivors."

The men took the tree into the mess tent and set it on a table. For those who hadn't seen an evergreen in years, it was a welcome sight. And the black dirt was a welcome change from the eternal brown dust of the desert.

Suddenly, there was a commotion at the doctor's hut, and the women began the shrill trilling ululation that marks momentous occasions. *The child!* Fahad jumped to his feet and dashed to the hut. A few minutes later, he emerged, holding a bundle over his head. The trilling grew; men danced and clapped. Fahad carried the bundle over his head to the wells.

Bulow emerged from the hut after Fahad had gone and walked slowly to

85

the communications tent. "It was easier than I had thought," he told Masters. "Many Arab girls have small hips, so I performed a Caesarian section under local anesthetic. The midwife had watched several of them and gave me some help. *Most* extraordinary."

"How is the mother?"

"Fine, just fine."

"And now Fahad has a son..."

"No, a daughter."

• • •

The camels were packed up, and the caravan made ready to leave. Fahad and his retainers mounted their horses. "Your turkey is most delicious, Major," Fahad shouted. "Your always-green tree is most wondrous. The works of Allah are great, indeed! A *fine* holiday custom you have. My tribe shall also observe it in celebration of Allah's miracles. Allah has been kind, Physician," he shouted to Bulow. "We *have* an *heir*. Your Promised One has much influence with Allah."

"*Allahu Akbar*. But a *girl*?"

"She will be married at the next feast of Ramadan," Fahad replied absently. "Her husband, whom Allah and I will choose, will be my heir. There is nothing new to that. This is better because I know what kind of man will succeed me."

"What will you tell your people about the ransom," Masters asked.

"You will give me a case of rifles and one of pistols, and a thousand cartridges for both. I will tell *them* Ached exaggerates. They *will* believe *me*." Then he offered his hand to Bulow, bending down low over his horse's neck. "You have helped Allah make a miracle, Physician-Priest. And now I must honor *you* with a gift." He squeezed his eyes shut tight and then opened them again with a radiant smile.

"Erect no pagan images, my learned *friend*. Teach of your Promised One to those who are interested—I will tell my *mullahs* and *imams* to leave your places and those who listen alone. Heal the sick as you always have, and teach your tongue so we might know of your world of flying machines and petroleum.

Fahad sighed heavily. "The days of salt wealth are numbered, I fear. Without salt, my daughter's tribe may not thrive, but with oil, she *might*. When she is of a suitable age, perhaps she can learn the healing arts in your schools and heal her people. Imagine," he added wistfully, shifting his gaze to a distant horizon, "a Bedouin wise in the ways that brought her to us." He looked again at Bulow. "*Ins'h Allah*."

"If it *pleases* God, Sheikh Fahad," Bulow answered, "If it *pleases* God."

86

The Crater

Al sometimes wondered what happened to that German…

Al Urton was one of those family friends that get called "uncle" by the kids, even though he was never really related. He'd met my dad during the war and stayed in touch after it.

Al was a corpsman with the 101st Airborne. They picked him and his outfit up in Paris in December of '44 and drove them until they got to a town in the middle of the Belgian woods called Bastogne. He was out on the perimeter on Christmas Eve, checking on some remote aid stations, and the Germans picked that very moment to try to attack the place again. So he's in his jeep and trying to outrun the tank shells, trying to get back into the town. He'd thought he'd got away, and then some artillery starts falling all around. Eventually, his luck ran out, and the jeep got thrown ass-over. He can only think of getting into some cover, so he jumps into a crater still warm from the shelling. The shooting got heavier, and he tried to bury himself in that hole. Then he heard some tanks around him and knows that it's Krauts, and he doesn't have too much a mind to be captured since the rumors of Malmedy were flying around...

The artillery's still falling, so it almost *has* to be American guns. There were a couple big explosions, and he passed out.

When he wakes up, it's snowing. He can hear some fighting somewhere, but right where he is, it's quiet. He gets up and starts to brush himself off and gets this feeling like he's not entirely alone. He turns around real slow like, and there, by God, he ain't alone, either. Sitting there all calm and collected, staring at Al, is a German in a black uniform wearing a headset. So Al looks at this German, looks around the crater. And the German doesn't move, just blinks. But there's something very wrong with this German he can't quite put his finger on. Then he figures it out...

This guy is sitting there with his left arm torn off. Not *blown off* or *chopped—torn off*. Pieces of the shoulder just shredded, hanging on him...

Al wasn't quite sure what to do since the German's got a pistol and he doesn't. But Al can move around, and he's sure the German's in shock. Then Al's training kicks in, and he offers the guy morphine. He said this guy had the clearest, gentlest blue eyes he'd ever seen, and the German just sits there while Al thaws the ampule in his mouth and sticks him in his wrist. Al thought maybe he'd try for the German's pistol but decided it'd be a mighty *stupid* way to get killed. So he did the next best thing. He gives him a candy bar. And the German just sat there and smiled and sucked on the frozen candy bar all glassy-eyed on morphine and shock and loss of blood, even if Al said there wasn't a lot of it.

Al offered him a cigarette, and they sat there, staring at each other and at the snow falling around them. The German couldn't really defend himself, much less take a prisoner, and Al could hardly take a prisoner back to his lines since he wasn't quite sure *where* he *was*. Well, Al wasn't quite sure how long he'd sat there watching this German, but some German tanks started to come back, and the American artillery walked back with them. Al dug himself deep into the crater again, getting all covered with mud and rocks and ice and shrapnel.

Then the artillery lifted, and everything got quiet. Al looked around...and there's the German, walking as calm as you please down the road, his headset still on his head. Al looks down the road and sees a German tank sitting there, so Al gets out of the hole, catches up to the German, and half-carries him to the tank. The guy in the tank just stares at him, and the wounded guy mutters something to him in German. Then the tanker waves at Al—waves at him to *go away*. They fire some shots into the air, so Al hightails it down the road and doesn't stop running until he finds some GIs at an outpost.

When I was in Germany, I'd tell him Germans of a certain age this story, and I'd buy them a beer. And they'd buy me two: one for me, and one for Uncle Al.

Rout Step

I got the basis of this story from my high school best friend's father, who told it something like this...

Some dates are remembered distinctly by where people were when they heard the "news." For my generation, those dates included Pearl Harbor and the death of Franklin Roosevelt. I remember Pearl Harbor well enough. We were getting ready for supper when the news came on the radio. My dad just stared at the speaker; my mother started to cry. My brother, four years older than me, jumped up and started talking about joining the Navy. *I* wondered how it would affect the end of the football season.

When Roosevelt died, my brother was in a Defense plant in California with a bad ear, and I was in Czechoslovakia, guarding a half million Germans, most of 'em were just walking home.

Yup. Just marching home at a rout step, and me and about two hundred other guys were trying to get 'em all on the same road. It didn't start out like that, though.

My tank platoon spent most of *our* war in Patton's dust, always trying to catch up to the leaders, mopping up one little pocket or another left over from the Battle of the Bulge. April of '45, we got grabbed up to escort a few hundred prisoners out of Third Army's rear area. They teamed us with about 90 MPs, a bunch of trucks, and an Italian field kitchen and started marching out of Czechoslovakia and back into Germany. Luckily we had a few CIC guys along that could speak German. When we started, it was pretty chilly, being *early* April, and it was raining some. There were a couple hundred Allies and my four tanks escorting and only about eight hundred Germans with about fifty miles to walk. Nobody figured it would be a lot of misery. Boy, I'd been wrong before, but *that* time, brother...

Anyway, about noon the first day, we bump into a convoy coming the other way, and we got told we had to take another road. We marched off at a fork down this little cart track. By then, it was raining pretty steady, and the track was ankle-deep in mud. Then we got word that another batch of prisoners would join our group at the next junction. *Another* cage was breaking up. *No sweat*, we figured...

Well, we added another six hundred prisoners to our bunch, but the guys *guarding* 'em said they had orders to rejoin their outfits. So now we've got close to twice what we started with, but no more *guards*. We try to map out the route we have to use and discover we've got about *seventy-five* miles to go. *Three* days, not *two*...

The first night, we found a meadow to rack in, and the Italians set up a mess and fed the prisoners while we ate K-rations. The Krauts spread out on the grass in the mud and wet and got what sleep they could. We weren't much better off...

The next morning somebody had decided they needed better organization than they had, and they sent out scouts to mark the route, and the Italians went ahead to find a spot for lunch. The trucks were starting to fill up with sick prisoners, and it was still raining, but we got started by mid-morning. Most of that morning, I was riding drag, and I could have sworn the pack of Germans was getting larger. My crew thought so, too, but they couldn't say just *how* they knew.

Just before noon chow, I stopped at an MP checkpoint and asked them about it. Yup, they said, it's getting bigger, all right. More cages added, I wondered. Nope, they say. They're just coming out of the woods and joining the line. War's gotta be over, I thought, if all they want to do is march home. The funny part was that a lot of 'em were still armed. They didn't really surrender; they just figured they were joining other Germans going home. We couldn't guard the whole road *or* the whole column, but they just marched along where we pointed 'em.

At chow, some bright boy figured that there were too many of *them* and not enough of *us*, so our best weapon was exhaustion. Keep 'em moving, somebody said. Stop 'em for an hour out of every six but otherwise, just have 'em keep puttin' one foot in front of the other. By then, our route was about a hundred miles, what with avoiding main supply routes, big towns, columns of refugees, bombed-out bridges, and pockets of German resistance. And we still had only two hundred guys guarding what the MPs now figured was about twenty *thousand* prisoners...and a fair portion of 'em were *armed*. And it was *still* raining. "Shove "em down the road," they said. "OK," I said. I was just a tech-sergeant, so I said *OK* a lot.

My driver struck on an idea that smacked of genius. The Eyeties were running out of chow, so they'd put out a sign telling the prisoners to deposit extra food at the mess tent, and it worked like a charm. My driver said to put up another sign telling 'em to deposit their weapons and ammunition. Hell, they're *Germans*; they follow orders. So we got a CIC guy to write down the words, and we painted it on a ration crate lid in crankcase oil, and you know what? They left their weapons. Of course, we had a German officer—a colonel, no less—standing *next* to the sign. *That* helped.

But we couldn't just watch 'em walk. We had to break up fistfights, brace bridges, chase rock-throwing civilians away, reroute around convoys, pick up their wounded and sick, try to see that everybody got at least *some* chow, disarm a few stragglers, and all this time try to stay as warm as we could 'cause it was *driving* goddamn rain and cold most of the time, with a little late-season snow thrown in for good measure.

After four days and three nights of this, we got word that the column's front had hit German territory. We were still ten miles or so away, and I could see a river of prisoners on both ends of the horizon just slogging through the mud. The MPs gave up trying to figure out how many prisoners we had and stopped when they hit a hundred thousand. They literally rolled out of the woodwork just to join us. And we still only had about two hundred guards with us, and none had slept more than an hour at a time since we started.

One night we stopped at a mess-and-rest tent, about a mile from the German border. It was staffed by a *Kraut* medical unit and the Red Cross, set up for prisoners who just couldn't go on and that we didn't have transportation for. They had pneumonia cases, influenza cases, and a minor outbreak of measles among the Hitler Youth that had joined the column. We'd had nothing but water and K-rations for four days. We were wet, cold, tired, dirty, hungry, and about deaf from the engine. An MP said he'd watch the tank while we went in to dry off. Inside that tent, they had a space heater that turned the place into a sauna, but dammit, I'd never been so glad to sweat in my life. We took off our wet stuff while the Germans just made room for us around one of the stoves, and we set our gear down to dry off. Didn't think much of it at the time.

In one corner, a German medic and a Red Cross woman were trying to deliver a baby, which in the nature of that sort of thing was kinda noisy, and the girl was Czech and couldn't understand a *thing* the Germans were saying. So this other Kraut goes over and starts talking to her in Czech. Well, we get curious and forget all about the heater, and everybody in that tent was watching this with a gasoline lantern over her head and the rain pummeling the canvas all around. Kinda spooky, ya know? Just a few minutes later, there's this big commotion over by the stove. We go back, and a couple Krauts are fighting a couple *other* Krauts over our weapons. We'd forgotten all about them, curse our luck, and one wiseass Kraut decides he's gonna restart the war. Well, a couple others don't like that idea, so a fight broke out, and in just a few seconds, there's some shooting, and the MPs come in. Well, we got our weapons back, and a couple prisoners have busted body parts and black eyes, and that tent had a couple new holes. The MPs hauled off the wiseguys, and we went back to the stove. A few minutes later, the baby decides it's time, and there's a new baby girl in the world.

Anyway, the rain let up a bit, and we head back down the road, following that *Feldgrau* river into Germany. At one crossroads, I see an old man and a couple of boys just standing there. The oldster was the boy's grandfather, and the kids were just too tired to keep going. It'd started to snow again, and the wind was picking up, so I hauled them aboard the tank. Well, once I got started, it was pretty hard to stop, so pretty soon, my tank was looking like the Joads coming across, with all kinds of people hanging off the sides, back, front, top. I put the gun tube in travel-lock and parked another ten guys on *it*. After ten days on the road in the rain and snow, we'd driven some two hundred miles back and forth and escorted about three hundred *thousand* prisoners back into Germany. I unloaded at a PW cage outside Nurnberg, and it was *then* I heard FDR was dead. I can't remember feeling anything but cold and tired.

So that was the end of the German Army, guarded by four tanks and two hundred guys. So I remember what I was doing when I heard of the death of Roosevelt: I was guarding a *Feldgrau* river, watching it flowing home.

Hold the Line

This story occurred to me in the middle of the night one night, and it still comes back to haunt me...

Cold. You never knew you could *be* so cold. But you're standing in a hole on top of a barren ridge in the dead of winter and wearing every piece of clothing you can put on.

And tired. Your eyes burn from holding them open, every inch of you aches from shivering. You're bone-weary, but you *know* you can't sleep. You lean back in your hole, adjust your belt, so the hooks don't dig into your back. You brace your knees on the other side of the hole. The cold from the earth sinks deep into your joints, but you've got to give your back and neck a rest from wearing this steel brain bucket. You watch.

God, it's dark, you think. And quiet. No birds, no wind, no insects, no nothing. Feels like you left the real world of life and light for this hole in a frozen desert on top of a ridge as long as three counties.

Out there, there's a million Reds who want to get you out of your hole, off your ridge. You can't hear or see them, but you *know* they are somewhere out in that desolate midnight blackness—massing, moving, plotting. You and a half million other guys in a line of holes stretching from sea to sea hold on in frigid darkness against a tide of humanity determined to throw you out.

What was that? Scuffling? Out to the left? You scan the horizon, looking out of the corner of your eyes since you can't see straight ahead in this pitch dark. You track with your rifle, tempted to pitch a grenade. It could be your listening post—you hope—or just your imagination. after a few minutes, you relax a bit.

In your hole with you is your best friend in the whole world that you just met last week. His name's Rawson, and he's from some little bullshit burg in Wyoming or Washington or someplace like that. Like you, he got drafted in '45 and had to stay in the Reserves after basic training and got called up for Korea. His older brother was wounded in Italy; his uncle was a merchant sailor in the Pacific, and his father made gear-hobbing machines during the last war. That's all you know about him, but he's your best friend because you've shared the same holes, dug the same latrines, eaten the same rations since you met. And right about now, you think he's the only friend you've ever had.

There it is again! That sound could be sneakers on frozen ground or padded uniform jackets against burp guns. You reach for a grenade and nudge Rawson. He peers in the same direction, sighting on that crested knoll off to the left, that little blind spot the Lieutenant was so worried about. You think about the LP out there, but not for long. If it's Chinks this close, their throats are already cut. The sound doesn't return. You wait, scan, shiver.

Your own dad was on Guadalcanal; he never talked about it. After the 'Canal, they brought him back to the 'States, and he spent the rest of the war at Camp Pendleton. All those places they wrote about in books and the papers—Mantanikau River, Tassafaronga Point. He never even brought it up. They didn't even tap him for the invasion of Japan, which, thank Christ, never had to happen 'cause we got the A-bomb and...

There! Again! *This* time there was movement and sound. You pull out the grenade again, yank the pin, cock your arm, and you hear a *whuff whuff whuff* over your head...

Shit. You drop to the bottom of your hole, clutching your pineapple. *Ba-lang!* The stick grenade goes off somewhere behind you. You and Rawson spring up. You pitch your grenade. Rawson opens fire with his Garand. The machine gun on your left fires where you throw, and the BAR in the next hole peppers the same place. A burp gun rattles, flashes dimly in the dark, another grenade *whuffs*, end over end, off to your left. You and half the platoon empty a clip at where it might have come from. Then nothing. Quiet, cold return, black midnight made blacker by the fury and suddenness of its violation and return. The cold bites your upper lip, tugs at your nose.

There's shuffling behind you, but you don't panic: too noisy to be a Red, *has* to be an American. "Willis; Rawson," your squad leader whispers just behind your hole.

"Yeah." "Yeah," you whisper back. He shuffles off again, duty done. He isn't such a bad sort. Your last squad leader was a real square, a retread from the last war, fought in North Africa. Real Audie Murphy-type 'till he stepped on a mine about three months back…

Clank!

God, what a racket. Out *there*...

Pop! Whoosh! "Trip flare!" somebody shouts. Gotta be a replacement.

As the lone trip flare arcs up, the platoon opens fire, and earth and sky seem to explode—bursting grenades flash. The fifty-caliber behind you fires, and every round socks your eyeballs as their shock waves pass overhead.

Both platoon thirty-caliber machine guns cut loose. Icy-red tendrils of tracer bullets probe the dark. Eight BARs and forty rifles erupt from the string of holes. Grenades and burp gun tracers rise to meet the curtain of fire from the ridge. Your rifle bucks and jumps as you fire, then you hear the *splang* of the empty clip and the *thud* of the bolt locking back. You fiddle with numb fingers, zip in another clip. The bolt snaps forward, catching your middle finger. Again. Rawson pitches a grenade. You come up with your rifle...

BOOM!

Artillery, you think, your ears still ringing and your head pounding, gravel bouncing off your steel pot. Real honest to God Chink artillery Christ they never use artillery, just mortars. I want to know what in the Hell is going on. When did *they* get artillery? Maybe it's a short round one of ours...

Shush shush shush. "Hit the dirt," you hear yourself yell. Now *that's* more like it. *Now* we're on familiar territory *now* they're using mortars, OK, *now* I know what's what...

Pweeet!

A whistle a Goddamn penny whistle for the love of Pete and now look at 'em Jesus Christ that must be half of goddamn China just come here to kick me the Hell out of this icebox of a country well just let me outta here, and they can have it *here they come.*

You see an amorphous blob of grey movement on the grey ground in the ghostly light of the grey-white flares swinging overhead and the flash and streak of red balls of gunfire. The firing gets louder, artillery crashes. You hug your hole and fix your bayonet *whuff whuff whuff* and get out the shovel *whuff whuff whuff* "Grenade!" *crack crack splang thud* another clip.

BAM!

"Aw shit, I'm hit *ahhhh...*"

A shadow appears right on top of you. He doesn't see you, but you see him. *Wham wham* and down he goes. This's the last of your ammo, and there's another Chink. *Blam splang thud,* "Rawson! You got ammo?"

"Yeah, here..."

"You hit..."

"Yeah, not bad, just stings some..."

"Christ, they see us now GET DOWN!" you yell as a grenade bounces off the back berm into the hole. You kick the grenade into your sump hole. It rattles down. You and Rawson, your best friend in the whole world, hug the opposite ends of the hole, the only hole in the world where you live...

BOOM! You find yourself halfway out of your hole, and Rawson is pulling you back in, still firing away. You can't feel your face. Where's your rifle? "You OK," Rawson shouts.

"Yeah, where's my rifle?" you holler back.

"Dunno. Go find one."

The noise seems to die down. Or you're going deaf. You crawl out of the hole, flashes and explosions all around. You crawl, defenseless, up the rise, past the fifty-caliber and the mortars, through a couple of cracks in the rock, to the platoon CP's hollow. The Lieutenant is shouting on the sound-powered phone, trying to get the artillery to lift and shift. Byers, the platoon sergeant, and the RTOs are taking shots at shadows popping up around them from the shadows.

"My rifle got lost," you shout at Byers. He looks at you, suspicious, and hands you a BAR and ammo belt.

"Get back up there," he shouts back. You scramble out of the hollow, crawl back towards your hole, your chest-rattling from the explosions around you. People jump over you while you're in a crack, catching your breath. You swing the BAR on the last two; they fall, motionless.

You decide this ain't that bad a place to be for a while, especially since it looks like you're overrun. Another flare goes up over the hilltop, punctuating that thought. A spike bayonet jabs down at you and misses your leg by at least half an inch. You swing the BAR up, squeeze the trigger. His head disappears in a dark mist against the flare-lit sky—time to *move*, maybe. And not a second too soon, because two grenades rattle into the crack. You swing around again, let fly a dozen rounds. Rawson is swinging his entrenching tool at somebody over the hole. *Whump* somewhere behind you... everything's in slow motion... quiet... you fire again... you're falling down... you fire another burst... they fall in a silent ballet... another flare goes up... but everything goes black...

• • •

Quiet again. Cold. Cordite, magnesium, and white phosphorous sting your nose. Around you are motionless lumps of bodies, grey in the dawn light. A corpsman shakes you again. You get to your knees and pick up the BAR, collecting your wits and strength. The corpsman walks off. Guys are sitting or standing around the holes, standing, and smoking. Some have broken out rations and are heating water for coffee. There's the sun, just under a cloud bank, a yellow sliver after the grey and red night.

You shuffle back to your hole, head ringing, body stiff. Rawson sucks on a frozen candy bar, a mittened hand wrapped in a bandage, sitting on the rim of your hole.

"There you are," Rawson says. "Sarge was looking fer you a few minutes ago. You OK?"

"Yeah," you say. "You all right?"

"Yeah. Corpsman gave me this a few minutes ago," he waves his bandaged hand. "Frag went straight through. Says I'll be evac'd this morning. Where'd *you* go?"

"Back to the CP," you say, turning to look back at the thirty yards that seemed so far last night. "Byers gave me this BAR, and I got caught in a little firefight on the way back, I guess; knocked me out. How'd *we* do?"

"Some of 'em got past the 3rd Squad over on the right, and *they* got caught plenty. Now we've found you, 2nd Squad didn't lose *anyone*. CP got mortared: Lieutenant's dead; Byers got a million-dollar wound."

And the line didn't break. You watch the sliver of sunrise, the clouds moving off.

Down in the bottom of the hole is your shattered Garand, the stock splintered by the grenade detonating in the sump. The metal is white-frozen in the mud at the bottom. The blood of the guy Rawson got with his entrenching tool mingled in the morass. The corpsmen are checking the motionless hummocks dotting the ridge. Some guys are dragging the dead away, eating, stacking weapons, drinking coffee.

You held the line for one more night. Your 2nd Squad would be one short tonight, but maybe they won't be back. But for now, you've got a BAR. And your squad is OK except for Rawson, who'll be gone for a week or so.

A breeze blows up from the south, warmer than the cold north wind of yesterday. Maybe today won't be so cold, you hope. Maybe tonight won't be so dark. Sometime today, you'll get a new best friend. But at least there *is* a today. *That* means there just *might* be a tonight and *maybe* even a tomorrow.

And you and thousands of other guys might still be out there, day after night after day, clinging to a chain of ridges and holes stretched from sea to sea, holding the line.

Big Gun

I got this story from a guy who said he worked on the Warren Automotive Command project in Detroit. It's just far-fetched enough; it could be true...

I remember hearing about a bloody great artillery piece that Saddam Hussein wanted to build to shell Israel. In the grand scheme of things, the aiming and accuracy are not that relevant. The technical challenge appealed to Gerry Bull, the designer, and the "gee-whiz" gimmickry appealed to Saddam. That it can't hit the broad side of a barn was pretty irrelevant, really. It's the *idea* that you can throw a shell as far as you can a small rocket. There's neither cost nor technical advantage to doing it. It's just for show.

Way back when the Earth was young—the mid-'50s—I was fresh out of engineering school and didn't *know* any better. I got involved with the firm that prime-contracted the Department of Defense project later called the Atomic Cannon. You gotta go to Maryland to see one now.

These big monsters were first deployed in *pentomic divisions* in Germany, converting a few 175 mm howitzer battalions to accommodate the guns. The pentomic division was a *bad* idea that got implemented for a few years. They consisted of thirteen maneuver battalions that were called a *division* because *kamikaze* was already taken and was *terrible* for morale. They had plywood dummies of the guns made up for crew drills. For months, they ran them around Germany, practicing emplacement, transport, all that kind of thing. Anything *but* shooting. Well, the press started to wonder why they never seemed to *fire* the damn things, and somebody got the notion that it was because the ammo for it was all nuclear, so it got dubbed the "Atomic Cannon." They were *right*, sort of.

The funny thing is there was never a *lot* of atomic ammo for it. Never built any more than a few thousand rounds of conventional and some instrument packages that never worked. The original intent was to test a replacement for the eight-inch and 175 mm guns. Since it cost twice as much to build as the other two combined, they scrapped the idea. But the project *did* reveal the Russian mindset and just *how* paranoid they were.

The Army ran those damn things all over Germany for nearly a year. One winter, the weather got *horrible* when one of the dummies was about a kilometer from the German-Czech border. The Russians—they used to watch American activity from the other side of the fence—had seen *the* big gun before, and they took all kinds of pictures of it. But like I said, the weather was *horrible* even for *Germany*: freezing rain and sleet for *days*. One day, about a kilometer from the fence, somehow the *front* tractor on one dummy got the notion to go in *one* direction and the rear tractor *another*. The fifth wheel sheared off the front, and the one in back just kinda gave way at the same time. Since they were sideways on a slope, the gun started to roll ass-over-teakettle down the hill right there in front of the Russians. It landed on its side at the base of the hill, practically intact.

That was the strongest plywood structure anybody ever built, I swear.

Well, the platoon commander was fit to be tied and *shot*, which he probably *would* have been. He orders up his radio jeep from the scouting section since it was about the only thing that could safely get down that hill and up again. It's *pouring* rain, and the slope is like grease, but that LT wanted to save himself the trouble of having to survey the damn thing.

Imagine an atomic cannon on a lieutenant's pay—even a plywood dummy. Yeah, right.

Anyhow, nobody tells the two guys in the jeep just *what* to do when they got down there. So this sergeant wraps a logger chain around a piece of the frame and drags this damn dummy atomic cannon diagonally up the hill.

It was about a quarter of the mass of the real gun, but like I said, that hill was *real* slick, and a jeep can get itself outta some bad scrapes. That sergeant used his front winch on stakes he pounded into the ground to get up part of the slope, but he just ground the gears for the most part.

Well, the Russians got an eyeful. One of their *best* intel analysts was on the border that day, and by the time he got there, the jeep was about halfway up the hill with the atomic cannon dragging behind it. Now, one thing we could never accuse the Russians of being was stupid, just unbelievably dense and arrogant. They "knew" all about the Atomic Cannon, or at least they were *convinced* they knew. But…they didn't know *anything* about the dummies.

They took all kinds of pictures and made all sorts of measurements from afar. Just as it was getting dark, the jeep was cresting the rise, and that damned German fog set in, cutting off the Russian's view across the fence. The gun crews managed to manhandle the damn thing back onto the tractors and got it back to the *Kaserne* by midnight. They spent the next day filling out a few hundred *feet* of paperwork on what happened. *Why* did they get so close to the Czech fence? *Why* was the dummy damaged? What were the dummy's *feelings* just before it took that plunge?

But that was *nothing* compared to the excitement back in Moscow. That

Russian hotshot analyst had seen all this stuff, and since he was the best the Russians had, he was supposed to come up with a brilliant piece of analysis for this latest development. So you know what he said?

First, you should understand that a large part of this Ivan's reputation came from his analysis of US and German artillery. Since the trend then was towards *rockets*, he figured the game was changing, but he didn't really have the *background* for rockets. He *did*, however, have the knowledge to branch off into the burgeoning European automotive industry, and he apparently figured that this could be a real coup to keep his career alive for a little longer.

He reported: "American Jeeps are able to shift a hundred times their weight on uphill slopes."

And they *believed* him, too.

What some folks won't do to look smart.

Not Yet

I never knew there were so many shades of white until we got to Alaska for the training exercise in November of '74. I thought Alaska had trees and mountains, but the only trees we saw were scrawny little things, and the only mountains were on the horizon.

There were forty-five of us plodding across the frozen white waste that morning. We'd jumped in out of North Carolina into an Arctic storm two weeks before and had another week of frozen hell to go. The sun was just peeking over the horizon to the south, even though it was nearly eight. The helicopters had dropped us off two hours before and were to pick us up six hours later.

Nobody remembered who *first* heard *shush-shush-shush...* the unmistakable sound of mortar shells. No one later recalled who shouted *INCOMING!!!* first.

Some guys were already diving for the ground when they hit.

BLAMBLAMBLAMBLAM!

The mortarmen couldn't have straddled a target better if they'd tried.

One round came down between the point and the front of the platoon. Another in the rear; one landed on each flank. The fuses were set at super-quick, so they went off right on the crust of the snow, with a maximum fragmentation effect.

Not yet.

What? *Who* said that?

First thing I remember after the explosions, I was face down in the snow, and I felt like I'd been kicked in the back. The next *I* knew, there was a whole lot of hollering. "CEASE FIRE CEASE FIRE," Lieutenant Bill hollered uselessly into his radio mike. *His* set was on the company frequency; *mine* was on Range Command's frequency. Tony Bill was one of those lucky guys who still looked like a little kid after he started shaving and would probably die an old man with a boy's face.

I got to my feet and shucked my ruck 'cause it felt hot. Radio parts fell out when it fell. The PRC-77 was designed for a lot of abuse but couldn't get hit with a 4.2-inch mortar fragment at ten meters and still work. But it stopped that frag from killing me. At least it didn't die for nothing. "Raise Range Command," the lieutenant yelled at Owens, his moon-faced RTO.

"Yassuh," Owens replied in his broad Alabama accent, his voice shaking with cold and shock.

"Hell, raise *anybody*," Sergeant Smith shouted. Platoon Sergeant Smith did three tours in the Southeast Asia Games and had a little more self-control than most of us just then. Eight of our nine NCOs had seen some firefights. A few guys just standing around with dumb looks on their faces, watching. A *lot* were lying in the snow, a *lot* were bleeding.

Those of us that could still do anything started shuffling around the AO, looking for casualties. Doc Tippie, our Medic, had found his first patient, Randy Buhler, a former machinist from Albany. Buhler was unconscious, a fragment having torn him open from knee to the sternum. Doc had bandages, aspirin, and iodine to treat him with.

Steve Acosta was screaming. A round had landed practically on top of him, ripping off one arm and the best part of a leg. Juan Morquetcho held Acosta down while he flopped around, blood splattering all over the multi-hued white snow. Steve was a giant lumberjack from California, and Juan was just a little squirt from southern Florida.

Up by the point of the platoon, Sergeant Morenzi tied a tourniquet to Dave Palmer's leg. Palmer was a skinny, goofy-looking guy from Queens. Now his left leg was gone just below the knee, his right foot was mangled, and he had fragments in most of his lower body. Palmer was our platoon sniper and alternate RTO. Except for a strained back, *he* should've been carrying my radio. Morenzi was our weapons squad leader, a quiet, unassuming NCO. He tried singing but spat out some blood through a hole in his cheek and gave it up.

Ernie Nash was in the middle of the platoon, an amiable machine-gunner just married a week before we came to Alaska. He was from Ohio and had been my roommate before getting married, though we never got along too well. Ernie had fragments through both lungs and was spitting frothy blood out on his parka. He didn't say anything, but he had a real strange smile on his face.

Ray Noller, second squad fire team leader from somewhere in Minnesota, was dead; most of his head was missing. So was Chris Nenning from Las Vegas. Nenning had caught a single frag in his chest that bored through and buried itself in his rucksack. Thirty-one guys had wounds of some kind, six of them what Doc called *serious*. That left twelve that could actually do something.

Owens tried and tried to get in contact with the outside world. He built a dipole antenna and chopped a hole in the ice (three feet down to solid earth) to make a better ground, but *nothing* worked. We wouldn't be missed for at least another six hours, we figured. Doc said that'd be too late for at least three of us. "Well, they'll start *looking* for us," somebody said.

"Look around," McGrath, our Alaska State Guard guide, told us. "Can you see the horizon?" We looked and looked but we couldn't. Sky and earth had merged in the same multi-hued mass of white. "Whiteout," McGrath declared. He tightened a bandage on his knee. "*Nobody'll* fly in it. Even if we raise somebody, there'll *be* no medevac. Do we even really know where we are?"

"Sure," the lieutenant pointed out on his map. "Right *here*."

McGrath didn't even look. "If we got hit by mortars, *sir*, then we'd be at *least* three clicks (kilometers; a little short of two miles) south of where we're *supposed* to be. They may not even know where to *look* once they *start*. Sir."

The lieutenant studied the map for no evident purpose. Without visible landmarks for orientation, it might as well have been a map of the Moon for all the good it did us. The lieutenant finally said, "I've got *two* dead and thirty-one other casualties *now*. By the time the weather lifts, I could have *forty-five dead. We* have to do *something*."

"We can send a detail due west to Border Road," McGrath said. "It runs the length of the Fort's western boundary. They hit the road and turn north or south, and they'll either find the Main Fort area or the State Guard post." Somebody did the math and figured we could spare four guys to walk the escape azimuth to the road and find help. The rest would dig shelters, keep watch, and try to keep the rest alive. Guess who got nominated to walk?

We left two of our rucks and all our weapons behind. We all had a compass, water and rations, and a flashlight. They figured we had about six hours to hump about forty clicks (just short of twenty-five miles) and bring back some help, or the rest of the platoon would probably freeze to death.

• • •

Al Mock led off, paced out a hundred meters on a compass bearing, and stopped. Stu Wainwright followed him, went a hundred meters beyond Mock, and stopped. I followed Wainwright, went a hundred meters beyond, and stopped. Phil Jacoby followed me, went a hundred meters out, and stopped. We repeated this, moving last to first and following the compass bearing, again and again, and again. With one man on pace, like normal land-navigation, our course would tend to swerve wildly on the slippery, treacherous ground, especially since there were no landmarks. *Two* guys on-line would still bend. Three might tend to veer around the center. But *four* guys could move across that featureless desert of ice and snow forever as long as they all kept lining up on all *three points behind* whenever they stopped.

The wind whipped up; ice blew into my face. My upper lip had long before stopped feeling anything. My eyes started to hurt, my hands were numb, and my feet were a strange mixture of frozen and blister-painful. My teeth chattered, and my chin started to ice up under my snow mask. A rime of ice formed under my nose.

The wind picked us up off our feet from time to time because our parka skirts acted like sails, adding injury to injury with painful falls. With the wind, we were falling down about once every hundred yards. Old soldiers talk about the wind in Germany and Korea. They call it the Hawk 'cause it screams in your ears as the wax freezes. I *heard* it scream, all right. It was saying: "You fool! *What* are you *doing* out here? *Yooooooou fooooool...*"

The tundra is a weird place to walk because the surface is illusory. What looks solid can really be soft; what looks rough may be glare ice. I'd set a foot down, try my weight, get about halfway up, and BANG! My elbows and knees started to bleed before I was out of sight of the platoon. I strained my groin with every slip and *every time* I broke through the ice. I stopped trying to fall after a while and found it was a little less painful.

After a few cycles, we remembered that this really WAS a desert, and we needed a *lot* of water. So every time we completed a cycle, we'd take a swallow of water. The stuff was bitter on the already-cold mouth, even painful, but those double-insulated Arctic canteens kept it wet. The best piece of equipment the Army ever bought, in my estimation.

The *worst* was those damn Arctic boots. Some nitwit thought that Arctic boots should be made out of solid rubber, and he sold the notion to some *other* nitwit in the Army. To top it all off, the hammerheads added an air bladder around the boots. Then they gave *us* the damn things. They're probably just great if you're standing in one place or walking a sentry beat, but for light infantry humping across Arctic waste, they're the worst *possible* footgear…because…

When you walk, your feet sweat. When you walk a *lot*, your feet sweat a lot. When you're *Infantry* on the *hump*, your feet sweat like Niagara Falls. Guess what happens to all that sweat when it's thirty below? You guessed it—it *freezes*. And so do your feet, socks, long underwear, pants liners, pants, and pants overcover as the sweat wicks up. After a few hours of this, you're carrying an extra *ten pounds* of frozen sweat on your legs that would just evaporate if you wore regular, rational footwear. So we kept humping with frozen legs, four hundred meters at a time. It was OK, though. After a few hours, we couldn't really feel our feet, anyway.

I had a kind of personal odometer at the time. After so many clicks, I got a pain in my knees. After so many more, it radiated into the hips, then into the gut. Out there, I was so damn cold, I'm not sure I was even thinking about it. I just hurt all over.

• • •

It was dark by the time Wainwright found a marker and waved at us to come up to him when he saw it. Up there, they've got a most marvelous system with signposts and mile markers up to twenty feet high with little strobe lights on them. We'd been marching for *hours,* but we couldn't *think* about *time*. It had long before stopped having any meaning. Our lives had become only shuffling, cold pain. The brain starts to act funny when you hurt that much. It starts to decide stuff *for* you, and it determines that breathing is essential, but digestion is not. Our guts were as hard as bowling balls with all that water in them. "South to Main Fort," I suggested.

Without discussion, we took a bead on the next signpost down. We didn't talk because it was all we could do to keep humping. Talking or thinking about what to say would take too much energy. In that kind of cold, anything you do expends energy. Just standing still requires an awful lot of the human body when it's thirty below outside. When you're trying to hump at six to ten clicks an hour, you'd better have an *awful* lot of energy stored up. *We* didn't, but we kept going.

We trudged from marker post to marker post until we saw a building with lights in it. Mock hammered on the door until a guy came and opened it. I will always remember that blessed blast of heat that slammed out of that forty-degree garage. We all ducked inside and shut the door. The building's CQ had let us in and stood there with his hands on his hips and a cigarette in his mouth, just gaping at us. We must've been quite a sight. Later we found out that the blood had wicked from our knees and elbows while they still had blood in them. Our whites were half-red by then, and we fairly stunk of blood. It was the *blood* that stunned him.

Jacoby started babbling an explanation first, and we all just kinda joined in. That CQ just stood there looking at us from one to another trying to make out what we were saying with our mouths frozen. I never realized how much you need to feel your tongue to talk until that moment. But even if we had been physically fine, we wouldn't have made much sense.

Finally, we got thawed out enough so he could understand us, and the CQ called the MPs and the medics. He opened the garage door, so we wouldn't get *too* unthawed before the medics came. The MPs took *one* look at us and called Range Command and our CO. The medics came and called the State Guard and the chaplains. Finally, after about an hour and saying the same

105

damn thing five different times, our Company Commander showed up, and *then* the fecal matter hit the rotary impeller.

Stuff always started happening *fast* when our Old Man started hollering. He'd walked from Hungary to Germany as a teenager in '57. He wasn't about to take any crap from anybody as long as his people were in peril. Range Command got some Snow-Tracks to come around, and the State Guard went out to find where we hit the road. Then they put the four of us in Snow-Tracks and sent us out after the platoon. You see, the Army *reasoned* that we knew where we were going and were naturally the rescue expedition leaders. Being one of the rocket scientists in the Army, I was authorized to drive a Snow-Track.

I got in one after leaving that blessed heat and started to drive. Snow-Track heaters have exactly two settings—off and furnace. The Medics said it wasn't a good idea for us to have it on in the enclosed Snow-Track cabins, so we left the floor vents open to keep my feet frozen until they could get my boots off. I was with the chaplain, a vivid, solicitous soul who had a most lovely whistling voice. After an hour of driving, I turned to him and said: "Padre (all chaplains get called "padre" regardless of denomination), I haven't felt my feet since this morning. I can't drive this thing anymore." Only part of that was true. I could feel *parts* of my feet, and they hurt *A LOT*.

"OK, son," he said, "let *me* at it."

"You ever drive one?"

"Nope, but you can't either."

I never heard anyone make *so* much sense in all my life.

• • •

When we finally found the platoon, Acosta, Palmer, and Buhler were dead, and Nash was nearly gone. Everybody else was about frozen solid and buried in the snow and ice to get out of the wind. Blood freezes bright-red, you know, and when it freezes, it stops flowing. A lot of the less seriously wounded would've bled to death if it hadn't been so damn cold.

We bundled the survivors into the tracks. The Chaplain, the medics, and the four MPs with us were the only guys out there who could handle the dead. They tied the black bags to a Snow-Track roof and headed back to post. The sun was nearly down again by the time we got there.

Our ordeal lasted a little over thirty hours.

They cut my uniform off at the hospital, stuck a bunch of tubes in me, and then dropped me into a whirlpool bath. Two days later, I woke up as the doctors were hugger-muggering about my feet: still no circulation below mid-calf. They did some pretty radical stuff—for the time anyway—to save my feet. I'd already lost the better part of two toes when they peeled my socks off. I spent the next two weeks in the hospital, answering all the questions everybody put to me.

In time, they managed to put together a picture of what went wrong. We had been at the far edge of a vast training area that doubled as an impact range, just a little south of where we were supposed to be. We were behind schedule. The mortars fired at Charge 1 (the minimum) to set their baseplates ahead of schedule. Still, under normal conditions, they shouldn't have hit us. The Army's insistence on wide safety margins should have put the mortar impact at least two clicks south of us. But a notorious high-level wind picked up those low-velocity mortar rounds and pushed 'em well beyond where they should have gone, right on top of us.

But there is still a mystery that has never really been resolved. Thankfully for Army bureaucratic nonsense, they do keep good records. We know from the communications logs that the mortars got a cease-fire from Range Command about impact time for the rounds. But who sent it? *My* radio got knocked out, and it was on the range frequency; the other one wasn't. Did they send the cease-fire before the frag hit me? I can't remember. I didn't send it *before* we got hit, I don't think. Range Command said they heard a cease-fire on the range frequency *and* said they didn't know the mortars had fired early. No one to date has come up with a reasonable explanation, though I've heard *many* theories. The most likely was that the mortar's fire direction center heard the firing off-schedule and sent the cease-fire. When all the screaming started, and all those officers got relieved, they just never said anything. That seems probable.

I remember all that blood on the snow. I remember Ernie Nash's smile the last time I saw him alive. And I distinctly recall thinking that the commie bastard that sold the Army those boots should be sentenced to wearing them for the rest of his life. I get reminded that I once got *too* cold for *too* long in every draft, every over-air-conditioned room, every open refrigerator, and every Midwestern winter.

And I remember the voice that told me…*Not…Yet.*

D-Day

If you've read this far, you know where this story came from.

My grandfather read the story about the invasion of France in the newspaper. He had been with Geronimo on his last foray off the reservation and had just turned ninety-five. Ancient for an Apache.

My father was then a hired farmhand in Montana, working 14 hour days six days a week for fifty bucks a month plus room and board. He was forty-one.

My mother was separating spider silk for optical crosshairs in a little sweatshop in Reno, Nevada. She was forty.

My uncle was in jail for nearly killing a store owner who refused to extend any more credit. He was thirty-eight.

After four day's tracking across the Egyptian desert, I finally caught up to a guy who'd knifed three prostitutes in a Cairo brothel. He was twenty. I was nineteen.

My sister died in childbirth in a trailer that passed for a clinic on the Reservation on that day. She was fifteen. The father of her child, also fifteen, was a stevedore in Washington and didn't know about it until over a year later.

So what do *I* think of the Normandy invasion? All these years later, I still get all choked up about it.

Bluffing

0520 Hours

Robineaux peered at the wall of fog and mist ahead. Somewhere in that soup, twenty or more Japanese ships—maybe *two* battleships—were heading south at twenty-five knots. The Japanese had pulled the American fleet carriers, battlewagons, and cruisers of Halsey's Big Blue Fleet away from the beaches with *another* fleet.

A chance US submarine patrol spotted the Japanese ships coming down the straights towards the beaches just five hours before. The trouble with such reports was that you had to throw out half and double the remainder to be accurate. The trick was knowing *which* half to discard. The nearest American fleet big enough to counter them was seven *hours* away; the nearest supporting fleet carrier *five* hours out of range.

"Radar, this is the bridge," Robineaux called into one of the voice tubes that lined the bridge railing.

"Radar, aye."

"Range to target?"

"One-two-oh-double-oh."

"Very well. Give me marks at five double-ohs."

"Aye, aye, sir."

"Captain Mirren," Robineaux called behind him, to the captain of his destroyer/flagship, the *Hopper*, "How wide's the strait?"

Mirren consulted a chart. "At estimated intercept point, ten thousand yards."

"The bottom?"

"At least a hundred fathoms."

Robineaux raised his binoculars. The mist got closer, but no clearer. *I know how narrow the waters are when I meet him,* Robineaux thought, *and the Jap doesn't even know I'm here. About the only advantage I have.* "Time to intercept?"

"Forty minutes, thereabouts."

"Very well." Twenty minutes. It took about that long to change the whole course of the war at Midway. Robineaux had been there, commanding a cruiser in the *Hornet*'s escort group. *Finally,* he'd thought then, *maybe we can win this.* Six months later, his cruiser was on the bottom off Guadalcanal. Then he got command of a destroyer division on the way to the Marshall Islands. He was promoted to Rear Admiral just before he got command of one of several amphibious groups and their escorts in the Philippines.

Twelve thousand yards north in a dense fog and closing fast, was the *biggest* Japanese surface fleet he'd ever seen, and only the *second* he'd *ever* seen. *If I had the sense God gave geese, I wouldn't be here, either.* Five hours before, the CinC had given Robineaux *freedom of action*, which meant he could save his command and as much of his mission as possible. Robineaux could have told the transports, jeep carriers, and inshore support ships to turn tail and run, leaving the Army alone on the beach.

Robineaux glanced aft. Five more destroyers steamed in line at five hundred yard intervals behind his flagship. *Benson, Tuller, Griffith, Paige, MacDonald.* Newer ships, untested in surface combat, named for influential captains, admirals, and sailor heroes. Behind his column and four thousand yards to the west were six destroyer escorts under the command of Captain Adam Gravelic, an Annapolis classmate. He'd raised his flag on a ship called the *George Lee*, named for a Yangtze gunboat skipper. Robineaux knew none of the other names. And bringing up the rear was a rocket-throwing LST named for a county in Michigan, pressed into service to provide some more show of force.

I wonder if they'll ever run out of names for destroyers and DEs. Or if, today, they may get a few more. We either get a ship named after us, or we get forgotten. Robineaux's "fleet" was all there was between the pride of the Imperial Japanese Navy and the transports and small escort carriers that supported fifty thousand GIs on the beach.

And Robineaux's nerves...

0555 Hours

"Dennis," Robineaux called behind him. Mirren came closer to the bridge rail where the Admiral stood. "Did I call it right? Am I asking *too* much?" The Navy had pulled the carriers and fast escorts away from Guadalcanal back in '42 when they had no choice. They left a handful of destroyers and cruisers to fight the Tokyo Express and the superb Japanese torpedoes. At first, Robineaux was ordered out with the carriers, but after two months of desperate fighting in those restricted waters, he and his ship were sent in. He lost his ship and nearly his life to the cold sea in his first and (until now) only surface action. He tried not to feel too bad about it; four other skippers lost their ships that night. The Japanese shelled the beaches the night he lost his tub *and* the night after.

"Not *my* play to *call*, Vince." Mirren had been the second-string quarterback in the Class of '22 when Robineaux was the lead signal-caller in the Class of '20.

"I'm *asking* how *you'd* call it." Robineaux turned slightly.

Mirren scanned the admiral's face briefly, then shrugged and looked away. "They *could* have a counter-invasion force," he answered at length. "Land troops behind the Army, expecting us to run. I'd have done the same thing."

"Thank you," Robineaux said, comforted but not relieved. "I'll be asking a *lot* of you and your ships this morning." Mirren was also the destroyer division commander.

"Yessir."

0600 Hours

"Bridge: radar. One-one-five-double-oh and closing fast."

"Ye*oman*," Robineaux called, and a signalman stepped forward.

"*Yes*sir."

"Signal to the task force. Command by TBS, otherwise follow the flagship."

"*Yes*sir: TBS or follow the flag." The rating left the bridge.

Robineaux watched over the open bridge combing as the forward gun crews readied their guns, removing rags, grease cans, tools, and paint from the turrets. Around him, antiaircraft crews greased pivots and tracks. Gunners pulled tampions from barrels. A detail nailed the anchor chain to the deck and covered it with canvas. A glancing hit could turn the chain into a whip, slicing huge chunks off the deck.

"CIC: bridge."

"CIC, aye."

"Take your plots from the radar repeater. Won't have time for visual confirmations when they break through the fog."

"Aye, sir."

He watched a torpedo crew behind the bridge pivot and test their tubes and saw the mess crew throw garbage over the side. Lifelines were being strung on the deck.

0610 Hours

"Bridge: radar. One-one-five-double-oh."

"All hands, this is the captain," Mirren said into the intercom. "Set battle stations surface condition one. Close all watertight doors; close all vents and stacks, main funnel on full draft. Main battery set armor piercing. Torpedoes set pneumatic launch and contact detonation. *All hands, man your battle stations.*"

The klaxon *whoop-whooped* throughout the ship as men dashed to their stations. Helmets were strapped down, life jackets cinched in. Disembodied, metallic voices on the tubes and intercoms, the TBS annunciator, and the radio repeaters told the world what they were doing, what they saw, what they wanted, what they had. Faceless men in a faceless void, embodied by speakers, receivers, and funnels.

"Sky-One mount *ready*," a voice intoned.

"Condition one *set* in forward power room, five-zero kilowatts on stream from forward..."

"CIC condition one *set*. Targets at one-one-five-double-oh, *two* columns..."

"Quartermaster McVey on helm..."

"Forward engine room *set* to condition one, full power available at one-eight-zero revolutions..."

"Galley fires extinguished, fuel lines shut and drained..."

Robineaux could vaguely hear—or *thought* he heard—other ships as they prepared to meet the enemy. He cinched down his helmet with the two stars emblazoned on the front and took a dab of the white flash-burn cream from a can passed around. Few of the sailors in his little fleet had been in a surface action, he thought as he spread the paste on his face, and even fewer had seen daylight surface combat.

But all that would change very soon.

I should be down there in the Combat Information Center, where I can see the whole situation. But then the men wouldn't see me, might wonder what that SOB-admiral was doing while they were getting shot up.

No. The bridge is the boss's place, especially when he doesn't WANT to be there.

0619 Hours

"Range one-one-oh-*double*-oh."

Through the mist, Robineaux could see the dim outline of ships, dark gray shapes against the light gray fog, off to the right side of his battle line. *We have been in their torpedo range since before we got them on radar, and they won't be in ours for another two thousand yards. Something about that rankles...*

"Yeoman!" Robineaux called.

"Sir!"

"Signal to CinC Fleet from Task Force one-one-point-four: Enemy in sight at." he glanced at his watch "oh-six-one-niner hours, and give our position."

Robineaux thought about the next phrase carefully. *Might be important at my court-martial... "Need help God's sake come quick.* Robineaux. Send *that*."

"Yes*sir.*"

Robineaux picked up the TBS receiver. "Flag to Gravelic: Execute phase one. Good *luck*, Gravel." Robineaux thought of the taciturn Gravelic; they had been ensigns together on the old *Pennsylvania*. Gravelic's wife, Louise, was Robineaux's daughter's godmother.

"Gravelic to flag:" came the reply. "Executing phase one. Good *luck*, Frenchy." Robineaux barely passed plebe-year French, despite his name. "Frenchy" became the Academy nickname that stayed with him.

The plan was simple: Robineaux and the destroyers would make a box pattern ahead of the Japanese columns, hopefully slowing them down and causing confusion. They would barrage the leading Japanese ships with torpedoes and a flurry of five-inch gunfire faster than the Japanese could reply. Gravelic and his smaller, more lightly-armed destroyer escorts would run parallel with the Japanese column, hug the coast, harass with torpedoes, and *maybe* pick off the odd cripple. Meantime, the escort carriers would launch their Avengers as soon as the fog lifted. *Might work. But enough bluff to save the beaches?*

"Set course zero-niner-five, Captain Mirren," Robineaux called. "Flag to task force: *follow the flag.*" The destroyer turned ponderously to the right. The gray targets shifted from the *Hopper*'s starboard side to port. *Crossing the T, if we were in school. Mission or men...freedom of action...mission or men...which to save...which to sacrifice.* He looked aft to Gravelic's column of destroyer escorts as they executed a classic "Scheer," or turnabout in line, where the aftermost ship becomes the leader. *If only this were school.*

"*Wayne County* to Flag," the TBS announced, "Targets in range."

Robineaux started. *Huh? They're still...no, wait.* The LST's hundred-plus barrage rockets outranged everything else in Robineaux's fleet, even from the back of the line. They may not have been able to do a damn thing and wildly inaccurate for ship-to-ship work, but their spread could cover three football fields, and they did have those new ground-penetrating rockets that could plunge through a deck...*maybe*...

Lieutenant Boyd, the young Reservist commanding the little converted landing craft, had been excited at the idea of participating in a fleet action. His uncle had fought at Santiago, and his father had been in WWI. *He near burst his buttons when I told him at the briefing a few hours ago. He'd nearly given up hope to see "real" action in this war.*

"*Wayne County* to Flag: Request permission to fire."

Well, son, here's your chance. "*Fire at will.*" Robineaux turned and raised his binoculars to look. A small gray line on the water seemed to erupt in flame. "Have a look, gentlemen," Robineaux said. "A sight you'll *never* see again. An LST in the battle line." Streaks of red and yellow shot through the gloom as rack after rack of rockets burst across the gray sea. Dull BOOM!s followed by flat ripping rolled across the ocean.

Robineaux turned around to look at the enemy ships' dim gray shapes, just to see what would happen when the rockets struck home. Small fountains were barely visible through the fog near the second in line. Then there were two, four small explosions on a gray shape. *Hits!*

"Flag to *Wayne County*: Four hits on target two. Now clear away." *Get a good spot to hide in. You can't keep up with us; you have to turn your whole ship to aim. You have no armor and not a chance of surviving more than one or two small-caliber hits. Now run away and hide, son, like I want to...*

Another shape appeared in the gloom. It was bigger, *much* bigger. "Range niner-five-double-oh."

"Looks like a *cruiser...*" someone said.

Two red dots appeared on the gray shape. "Target three *firing*," a voice tube from the main director called out. "Range niner-five-double-oh."

For what we are about to receive, may we be truly thankful...

"Torpedoes off port bow!" an anonymous lookout shouted.

"*Hard left rudder*," Mirren ordered the voice tube. The bridge crew held railings and furniture as the deck pitched to the right and the bow started left.

"Flag to task force;" Robineaux called on the TBS, "torpedoes to port—evade to port." Closing the range would throw off their aim faster.

The sighing of shells rent the air. Two splashes rose from the leaden sea on the far side of the turning battle line. Two torpedoes, then two more, bore in towards the line. "Torpedoes dead ahead." The deadly missiles swept towards the flagship, passed the bow and the stern almost simultaneously. The closest was ten yards off. *Combing, if this were school.*

"Resume course zero-niner-five, Captain Mirren," Robineaux called. "Flag to task force: follow the flag." The destroyer heeled over again, the spray splashing the bridge.

"Damage Control to bridge: Taking water at frames six and seven..."

0650 Hours

"Range eight-five-double-oh."

"Target one firing." Another gray shape emerged from the gloomy fog. *Five now...*

"Fog is lifting." Robineaux swept his binoculars from side to side. So it was. *At this rate...*

"Yeoman!"

"Aye, sir!"

"Flag to Carnival Four: If you're coming, make it now or not at all."

"Aye, aye, sir!" Carnival Four was the call sign for *Gettysburg*, the nearest escort carrier. They were tasked for ground support, not ship engagement. They had no torpedoes, just HE bombs, and canisters of Napalm.

Shells sighed overhead, much closer, and larger. Shells splashed on both sides of the battle line. *They have our range...*

"Flag to task force: make smoke and follow to course zero-four-five. Make all speed." *Have to throw them off. Smoke may hide the straddling splashes.*

"Fight your *ship*, Captain Mirren," Robineaux said, watching the enemy.

"Main Director," Mirren called into a tube. "Are you in range?"

"Range closing," a voice responded. "Two targets."

"Fire as you bear."

"*Standby* to *fire*," the director's voice was tinny on the ship-wide intercom.

"*Stand clear*." The boxlike gun turrets slewed in synchronization with the director high above the deck. *AWOOGA*, a horn sounded; *BLAM*, the guns roared. Concussion pressed temples and lungs, socked eyes. The ship vibrated. The other destroyers in the line joined in.

"Torpedoes: do you *have* a target?"

"Range extreme, but I *have* a target."

"Fire as you bear."

Whoop went the klaxon, and one at a time, four torpedoes shot out and splashed into the gray water. "*Torpedoes away*, straight and normal. Run time six-five seconds."

"Carnival Four to Flag: Launching *now*." The Avengers would be twenty minutes, at least.

Sighing shells passed overhead. *FOOM! FOOM!* They splashed the line with splinters, water, and concussion.

"Target one firing. Range eight-five-double-oh."

"*Splash* on target one. Fire for effect."

AWOOGABLAM!

WOOM, a shell landed just off the bows, showering the bridge.

"Torpedoes port abaft!"

"Hard left rudder!"

"Flag to task force: evade torpedoes to port."

"Target hit forward."

AWOOGABLAM!

WOOM, a shell landed off the port side. Robineaux looked to the enemy, then behind him. *Tuller* had been hit but was keeping station. The leading enemy destroyer had taken several hits but was maintaining course and speed, driving ever south.

"Damage control to bridge: Water coming in to forward fire room.

Flooding controllable..."

"Machine shop to damage control: get your asses in *here* if you think it's controllable. I've got friggin' Niagara *Falls* in here..."

0701 Hours

A tall tower-like structure loomed out of the gray fog. *Pagoda mast. Battleship or battlecruiser...Christ, what have I done...*

"Six-five seconds..."

"Target two exploding!"

The second ship in the Japanese line seemed to erupt in a ball of flame and spray, *again*, and a *third* time. Dull explosions flattened the sea around her.

"Set course to one-eight-five," Robineaux ordered. Got to stay ahead of them. *They're turning off our stern...calling my bluff...still headed south... avoiding me. Fight or flee...decide now...get word to the transports and the inshore ships to get the hell out... choose now...we can outrun 'em...we don't have to stay and fight at these odds...no one would blame me...*

"Course one-eight-five, sir."

"Very well. Flag to task force: follow the flag." *Stay ahead...keep moving...freedom of action... don't let' em down...*

Off to the west, enshrouded in fog, plumes of flame arched across the sea. *Son, don't YOU know when to hide?*

0720 Hours

"Carnival Four Air to flag: *Tally ho!*" Six pairs of Avengers streamed over Robineaux's battle line, descending to just above the waves. *Torpedo run? What in hell...?*

"Going in below the flack," Mirren observed, "*and* our gunfire."

"*Check* fire; *check* fire; *check; check; check*," the gun director called. *Wouldn't want to hit one of them ourselves...*

The planes seemed to pair off as they approached the Japanese ships. Puffs of antiaircraft gunfire appeared, the expended shells churning the sea below.

"They haven't *got* torpedoes," someone on the bridge said uncertainly, "do they?"

A thousand yards away from the Japanese line, the pairs were still boring in each pair on a different ship. Flak burst above and behind.

"Maybe not. But the *Japs* don't know that."

Eight hundred yards away, they should have dropped their "fish" and be pulling away, but in they came, prop wash raising white geysers of foam on the gray sea...

Five hundred yards and they were skimming the wave tops. Angry red tracers searched the sky.

"What in the *hell* are they *doing...?"*
Three hundred.
"Good jumpin' Jesus. Them flyboys are gonna ram!"
One hundred.
Skip bombing? Do they have the training, the fusing?
Fifty.
Dark shapes fell out of the bomb bays, and the Avengers pulled hard up and over their targets. Heavy splashes in the water, an explosion of foam, then...

"One! *Two* hits!" the director exulted. "Three... four, five...Christ, look at that!"

Two enemy ships slowed, then a third. One staggered and was visibly in trouble, going down by the bows. Another listed heavily. A third was aflame amidships.

But their battle line continued south, driving past.

"Carnival Four Air to Flag: here's the *ghost* of Torpedo Eight." Torpedo Squadron Eight, wiped out at Midway without launching a single torpedo.

"Flag to Carnival Four Air: bring it back again." Their Air Group commander had been a midshipman under Robineaux's tutelage while he taught at the Academy in '35. The flyer had a broken foot and was left on the beach when Torpedo Eight went to Midway.

Eighteen...nineteen, Robineaux counted... twenty... twenty-one Jap ships still afloat and headed south.

Robineaux trained his binoculars to where Gravelic and the DEs should have been. Traces of smoke, lingering mist, a flashing glimpse of a gray shape against the lingering coastal fog. *Call Gravel...find out how he's doing...as if that would serve any purpose but mine...he's at least as busy as I am...he knows what to do...*

"Course two-six-five, Captain Mirren."

AWOOGABLAM!

"Rockets landing. Hits on targets two and six..."

AWOOGABLAM!

0820 Hours

WOOM! An explosion shook the *Hopper.* Robineaux turned to look behind. *Tuller* was pulling out to the left, listing badly to port, her side ripped open from the main deck to waterline.

"Damage control, this is after engine room. Your patch just busted, and we're taking on water again. Christ, hurry *up...*"

Benson, just ahead of *Tuller* and behind *Hopper,* was fighting fires on her deck and still working the main batteries. Her torpedo tubes were engulfed in flames.

"Engineering, this is the forward power room. I've got a fire in here. We're gonna have to shut down for a while...Hurry up, guys...I ain't *got* enough extinguishers...."

Griffith, just behind *Tuller*, steered clear of the sinking *Tuller*. Two heavy shell hits had destroyed *Griffith*'s main director, and water pressure to fight fires was decreased by the loss of the main pump. Her rudder was jammed and was steering with engines.

"Engine room, this is the forward pump room. I can't get more than a few inches of suction, and I've got a whole lot of demand from aft...come on, fellas, get that line fixed..."

Hopper had been hit amidships and aft by small guns and suffered several plate-popping near-misses from heavy shells. Fire near the after powder room had silenced half her main battery for crucial minutes.

"Bridge, this is sickbay. We're full to capacity, and the mess deck is filling fast. I'm gonna start sending 'em to the wardroom..."

AWOOGABLAM!

"Target five firing. Range six-five-double-oh..."

"Rockets inbound..."

"Torpedoes on the port beam!"

"Hard right rudder!"

0920 Hours

"Come to oh-niner-five," Robineaux called. They had cut across the front of the Japanese line twice again in two hours and were about to cut across a third time.

"Carnival Five to flag: launching." Carnival Five was *Appomattox*, another escort carrier just reaching launching position.

Tuller had sunk. *Benson* and *Griffith* had pulled out of the line and tried to save themselves, unable to keep up. *Paige* and *MacDonald* had drawn up, but *Paige* was severely hit and had lost central gun direction and torpedo tubes.

"Bridge, this is damage control five. I've got guys trapped in the number five powder room and oil coming in. The hoist is stuck between decks. Get those extra torches down here, or we'll lose 'em sure..."

Hopper had been hit twice more. Her stern battery was silent, the aftermost turret and the after director lost. The ship was taking water in a half dozen places. Casualties had filled the wardroom and were now being laid out on the deck.

WOOM!

A heavy shell struck *Hopper*'s stern. *We're slowing.* "Damage control..." A loud screech came from aft. *If that's what I think it is, we're dead...*

"Port prop shaft's snapped, sir," Mirren told him. "Starboard shaft's without lubrication. Rudder's jammed." He added under his breath. "I'll signal for *MacDonald* to come up and take you off, sir."

"No need for tha ..."

KAWOOM!

Another explosion amidships threw Robineaux and everyone else to the deck. As they got to their feet, the sirens and alarms sounded. *Hit again. Heavy shell...*

"We'll *have* to get off, sir," Mirren said as he keyed the intercom. "All hands, this is the Captain. Abandon ship. I say again, abandon ship. Gunner's mates lay aft and get the depth charge primers overboard. Lower all boats and rafts. All hands topside. Bear a hand with the wounded. All hands abandon ship."

Robineaux descended to the main deck. He helped several men with life jackets, lowered rafts into the water, and did what every able-bodied sailor was supposed to do at times like that—help everyone else.

BLAM the guns of the other ships roared. *Hopper's* surviving main guns barked once again as dull rumbling shook through the ship. *Internal explosion, engine breaking loose, a frame giving way.* "*Abandon ship,*" the loudspeaker intoned. "*Abandon ship.*"

Robineaux went to the rail, unstrapped his helmet, and threw it over the side. *I sacrificed my command for no gain,* seeing *Gettysburg* in the distance, now open to surface attack. He knew of only two ships capable of action, and he could communicate with neither. And now he was leaving another sinking ship. He thought about the oily water about to envelop him with resignation, folded his arms over his face, and stepped off.

1011 Hours

"Admiral Robineaux!" a sooty and winded officer called out, walking around the masses of rescued sailors on the deck. "Has anyone *seen* the Admiral? Admiral *Robineaux!*"

"Over *here*," the corpsman shouted. "He's over *here*. Now, sir," the corpsman sighed to the wet, cold, bloodied, and exhausted admiral, stinking of oil. "*Be* a good sport, and let me get you below, or the doc will have my *hide*. They'll come to *you*, sir. Now come *on* below..."

Sometime between going into the water and climbing aboard *Paige*, Robineaux had done something painful and bloody to his mouth. He thought it was a broken tooth, but he wasn't sure. "I'm *fine*, corpsman," Robineaux told him through clenched teeth "I'm all right enough to get through the day. Now let me get up to the bridge and see what I can salvage outta this mess. I gotta get..."

"*Admiral,*" the sooty officer said, breathlessly rushing up to him. "*Sir*, I'm Jensen, executive officer. Captain Perd invites you to the bridge. And may *I*, sir, be the *first* to *congratulate* you."

Congratulate me for what? For losing not only my command but also my flagship...? Wrapped in a blanket, Robineaux and the corpsman followed Jensen up the ladder ways. They passed blackened faces streaked with white anti-flash cream, dripping with water and oil with bloodshot eyes in hollow sockets, their chests heaving for air, coughing up black phlegm and oil. The reek of seared flesh and burned hair mingled with smoke, cordite, and vomit, lingering over huddled groups of sailors long past caring. A blind sailor held a wrench on a hose at a stairwell landing while a one-armed shipmate tightened the coupling.

As he reached the bridge, Robineaux thought something was missing, but he wasn't sure what. Officers and men on the smoke-begrimed bridge pointed off to starboard. "*Admiral* on the *bridge*," a yeoman called.

"Sir," Perd said, getting up from the bridge chair. "Matthew Perd. *Your* bridge, sir..."

"*Your* bridge, captain," Robineaux replied painfully. "Just let me get word to the transports to pull the hook and..."

"But, there's no *need*, sir."

"What?" Then it struck him. What had been missing; the guns had ceased firing.

"They've turned *away*, sir. Turned back north. Started about ten minutes ago."

Robineaux seized binoculars from Perd's hands and trained them north. The menacing shapes of the Japanese ships had turned around and were headed back north, up the straits. "It started when Carnival Five was leaving, and Four was arriving again," Perd said. "Made it look like a real carrier air group had arrived, I guess..."

"You *did* it, sir," the corpsman said, holding Robineaux by the arm. "*You* turned them back. Now you just *come* with me..."

Robineaux slowly lowered the binoculars, watching the oily waters that surrounded his ships. Junk and boats studded the water. Rafts ardently paddled together. Lifeboats pulled with powered gigs. Oil and debris glimmered multihued on the water. "I wish it *was* me, son. But it was..." he was quiet again.

Benson, close abeam *MacDonald*, would be saved. *Griffith* was too far-gone and would be torpedoed as soon as the last of her wounded got off. Two Japanese ships burned a few thousand yards off. Of *Hopper*, there was no trace. *It was them. Not me. Not just me, anyway.* "Anything from Captain Gravelic," Robineaux winced at the little pickaxes digging at the side of his face.

"Over *there*, sir." Robineaux looked off to the northwest, where three DEs sailed in line on a bearing roughly towards the destroyers. One had damage to the bows; another was smoking from a hole in the stern.

"What ship leads?" Robineaux asked. A signal yeoman flashed the leading ship with his light.

"*Stewart*, sir."

"Captain Gravelic?" The whole right side of his head throbbed.

"Can't *say*, sir. Commander Mullen has taken command of the division."

"Mullen," Robineaux said quietly. "Mullen... Reservist, isn't he?"

"Coast Guard, sir," Perd offered.

"Yes, of course. Good man, as I recall." *Gravel...ah, Gravel... what have I done to you?* "Got a U-boat in the North Atlantic in, um, '42..."

"I believe so, yessir."

"Yeoman!" Robineaux called, using all the strength he had left.

"Yessir."

"Signal to CinC: Enemy turning north at" he looked at his wrist. Dumbly, he realized his watch had been lost in the sea. "Well, get a time. Will remain on station—get a position from the plot—until relieved. Sign it, Robineaux. That's all."

"Yessir."

"Well, look at *that*, will ya?" Robineaux turned to look at the western shore where the bridge lookout pointed. Streaks of red flashed as *Wayne County* fired once more at the retreating Japanese column. "I'll be a monkey's uncle..." the crew were saying, "if *that* ain't one for the books..." "I'll never say another evil word about Long Slow Targets again..." "Damn if she won't get the last hit in, too..."

Robineaux felt cold and very, *very* old. *An LST in a fleet action; outnumbered two-to-one and toe-to-toe with battlewagons... you got your battle, son, and you'll get a destroyer named after you. And we saved the beaches.* "Form a patrol line across the straits, Captain Perd," Robineaux said. "Have the DEs close up behind the destroyers." He looked out across the sea. "And have *Wayne County* fall in the patrol line."

"Yessir."

"When—*if*—Captain Mirren is found, I believe *he* is senior officer..." Robineaux felt faint. "And *now*, Captain, if I could please borrow your sea cabin..."

1950 Hours

"Signal from CinC, sir." Robineaux was lying down. The ship's doctor had given him morphine for the pain and packed the shattered teeth, but the fleet dentist would have to remove the broken roots.

"Read it."

"Congratulations, Frenchy, and all hands in your task force. Will arrive personally tomorrow. Signed Halsey."

Robineaux listened with numb detachment. He felt better after resting and getting cleaned up. His skin crawled from degreasing, the strong soap still wafting in his nose. *I'll have to write Louise about Gravel...*

He remembered a football game in 1925 when he and Gravelic had led *Pennsylvania*'s Palookas to victory against *Arizona*'s Animals. Halsey had been there, too, as an umpire. And there was the marathon poker game that followed when Robineaux ended up with everyone's money.

Including..."Robineaux to Halsey: How's your poker game?"

McLean House

Billy Dent scanned the tree-lined road, shotgun butt on his hip, muzzle in the air, finger near the trigger. As the war seemed to be ending, he was Headquarters Sergeant-Major and main bodyguard for the General.

It had been raining for nearly three weeks off and on in central Virginia. There were very few signs of spring, even though it *was* early April. Few birds, few blossoms, no squirrels chattering, and scurrying. The roads were rivers of mud that splashed up on the horse's chests, the men's boots, and mired the caissons, guns, and wagons in a knee-deep oozy grip. Teams snorted and struggled. Teamsters pulled and cursed and whipped horse and mule alike.

Ten yards behind Dent, General Porter, the General's chief assistant, rode alongside General Grant, who chomped a cigar. A troop of cavalry and staff followed. When Dent took the job as a personal bodyguard for the general, he admitted that he couldn't hit the ground with his hat when it comes to musketry. Because of that, the staff had got him a Greener 10-bore double-barrel shotgun that used the new-fangled metallic cartridges. He liked the additional stopping power the big piece gave him. With it, he could actually hit something other than air.

They passed row after line after knot of soldiers and cavalry in blue, dressing stations still doing brisk business. The General avoided the dressing stations with his eyes, puffed his cigar furiously when near. Old habit, the General had told Billy. His work in a tannery as a youth had sickened him to the sight or smell of blood.

Dent absently swept the countryside with his eyes. The area was slight rolling hills and mud-spattered fields denuded of trees and brush, gathered up for winter fuel. *Not much place for an ambuscade*, he thought. *Good place for a battle, though.*

The Army of the Potomac and the Army of the James had been in pursuit of the Army of Northern Virginia for nine days, and many soldiers had not slept *or* eaten in six. The men in blue serge were just as weary, cold, wet, and hungry as those in butternut and homespun that they chased and fought with every day since the breakout from Richmond.

But for every man in Lee's army, there were at least five in Grant's. As of that morning, Lee's men were cut off. The rebel's last route south had been occupied by the Union the day before, and their ration train had been captured by Federal cavalry.

Dent rounded a curve in the road and reined in, reflexively signaling those behind to stop. Some distance ahead was the six-building town of Appomattox Court House. On the outskirts sat a brick house with a wide front porch and a huge yard, surrounded by soldiers in blue. Outside the house, two horses grazed on the sparse grass. A Rebel sergeant with a Sharp's carbine stood on the porch. Dent spurred ahead. *Twitch, Reb, and I'll blow you to Perdition*; Dent lowered his shotgun muzzle slightly.

At that moment, the sun broke through the scudding clouds and cast a golden midday light on the sea of brown and red mud around the dull brick house with odd yellow trim. Hundreds of men looked up at the sun and grinned at the break in the weather. *That* meant a chance to dry out blistered and wet feet and light cookfires with dry wood.

Dent dismounted quickly. The Rebel sergeant and Dent glared at each other in the manner of bodyguards sizing up potential threats. Colonel Babcock, Grant's aide, waited on the brick house's front porch. He had carried Grant's last message to General Lee and had escorted him to this house. A civilian stood next to Babcock. Momentarily the General's entourage rode up. "Babcock," Porter nodded.

"They're waiting for you inside, sir," the officer replied. Dent took Cincinnati's reins as the General handed them to him and mounted the porch. Babcock introduced the house's owner, Wilmer McLean.

McLean was a Quaker who found himself living in the middle of a battlefield one Sunday morning in July of 1861. By the end of the battle—First Bull Run to Northerners; First Manassas to Secessionists—his house had burned to the ground. There was a *Second* Bull Run a year later, but McLean had left for another house he owned, where he thought the war would never find him again.

One by one, the officers entered the house—Grant, Sheridan, Porter, Ingalls, Williams, Merritt—tracking heavy mud up the steps and into the parlor. Colonel Parker stopped, scraped the worst of the mud off his boots, and entered.

A gleam of steel caught Dent's eye, and he saw the rebel sergeant cut himself a plug of tobacco from a large block. The rebel's uniform was clean but worn. "Say, Johnny Reb," Dent called in a neutral tone, "Trade coffee for fresh chaw."

The rebel looked at Dent blankly. "Fair 'nuff, Yank," was the answer.

Dent fetched a small bag of beans from his saddlebag.

Several of the General's escorts were boiling coffee and frying hardtack on cookfires in the yard. Dent cocked his head. "Smells like fresh mud. Join us?"

"*Hell*," the rebel grunted, casting a glance at the door, "*They'll* be a while." The men looked up as the two sergeants approached. "Got coffee and chaw to share," Dent said.

"Got fatback and crackers," one answered.

"Got peppercorns," the Rebel offered.

The men smiled. "Anybody with peppercorns' welcome to *us*. Amos MacFarland, Queens County New York."

"George Malloy, Hardin County, Tennessee," the rebel replied, tossing a small bag on the ground.

"Billy Dent," Dent offered. "I'm from the Army."

"And a *Regular*, b'Jesus," MacFarland exclaimed. "Dinna think there was a single one left."

"And it's a near-run thing *I'm* still about," Dent replied.

The peppercorns were unceremoniously ground with a Bowie knife blade on a flat rock and sprinkled on the fat pork, which was then chopped into strips, skewered on bayonets, and hung over the fire. The men watched the fire, chewed tobacco, spat occasionally. The coffee boiled.

A troop of Federal cavalry rode up at a gallop, and General Custer, blonde mane unruly under his flamboyant hat, rushed up the porch.

Coffee was poured into waiting cups. Dent skimmed off cracker weevils and dirt-scum with a gloved finger and watched Malloy do the same with his Bowie.

Cincinnati threw his head back, snorted. "*Easy*, boy," Dent cooed. "*Easy* now."

"Horse got yaws," the rebel Malloy asked.

"No yaws in our animals. Yours?"

"Some." The men turned back to the fire and the sizzling pork that dripped grease into the fire. Presently the skewered meat was passed around.

"Mm," Dent said after biting in. "Long time since I've had peppered pork."

"Been a fair spell since *I* had any vittles a'tall," Malloy grumbled as he chewed. "You'uns been chasin' us so hard we ain't hardly ate since we left Richmond." Silence greeted the remark, a courtesy extended to all for the etiquette breach—no mention of war while eating.

"Sorry," Malloy said at length. Dent smiled and nodded over his cup.

"Well," Malloy sighed. "Reckon this'll end it for *us*."

"I imagine that's so," Dent said.

"Had a mind to meet up with old Joe Johnston's boys, but..."

"The General *thought* that."

"Well, *hell*," Malloy sighed at length. "Got thirty acres of bottomland to get back to in Tennessee."

"I've my bookshop," MacFarland said into the fire.

"Suppose I *ought* to go back to school," another cavalryman said.

"I'm *not* goin' back to the mill," another added.

"And I go where the Army sends me," Dent offered.

"Well," Malloy drawled, watching the house, "This here's what it's all for, anyhow. The peace and the goin' home ag'in."

Wherever home is. Pa's dead now three years. Ma's with her folks in Connecticut, and I've never been there. Where do full-time soldiers go after the war's over?

Dent thought of the Sonora blooming green after a sudden rain, one of his earliest childhood memories of the Arizona Territory. *The Army's not a bad life as long as no one's trying to kill you. And no one tries most of the time.*

Officers emerged from the house. Dent and Malloy replaced their bayonets in their scabbards and led the horses back to the porch.

"Now there's a sight," Malloy said as the two Generals stood side by side, patrician Lee a head taller than shopkeeper Grant. The gentleman Lee immaculate in his best dress uniform; the merchant Grant in mud-spattered boots and a Private's coat with Lieutenant-General's shoulder straps.

So that's Marse Robert. He looked like he thought a Southern aristocrat should look: tall, arrow-straight, well-groomed gray hair and beard, clear eyes, spare of frame, and movement. Lee looked sad, striking his gloved hands together, looking down the valley. *Sad and weary.*

Dent then saw Captain Marshall—Colonel in Confederate service—as Lee stepped off the porch. Dent nodded at him. Marshall nodded back with a sad grin of recognition. *I am glad you have survived*, the grin said. Dent was saddened when Marshall went South.

Only a soldier could truly hate war.

"*Fall IN*," someone shouted, and in a great flurry of movement, the men formed serried ranks in the yard, cookfires forgot.

The two Generals-in-Chief shook hands, and the gray aristocrat mounted his horse.

"Pre-SENT ARMS." *Clunk-rattle-SNAP!*

The gray-clad general looked around him from his horse, took his hat off his head, and placed it over his heart as he rode away.

"*Fare* thee *well*, Billy Yank," Malloy shouted to Dent as he rode after his General.

"Fare *thee* well, Johnny Reb," Dent waved. "Fare *thee* well."

About the Author

John Beatty is a historian and writer in suburban Milwaukee, Wisconsin, and a US Army veteran of over 26 years of service. He has written several books and essays, magazine articles and has a blog at https//:jdbcom.com.